El Pa

AND THE GREAT SPELLING BEE

By **Marciano Flores**
Illustrated by
Mathew Flores

Published by Two Penny Publishing
850 E Lime Street #266
Tarpon Springs, FL 34688
TwoPennyPublishing.com
info@twopennypublishing.com

For permission requests and ordering information, email the publisher
at: info@twopennypublishing.com

ISBN: 978-1-950995-94-3

Library of Congress Control Number: 2023903521

FIRST EDITION

For more information about the author or to book him for your next
event or media interview, please contact his representative at:
info@twopennypublishing.com

Two Penny Publishing is a partnership publisher of a variety of
genres. We help first-time and seasoned authors share their stories,
passion, knowledge, and experiences that help others grow and learn.
Please visit our website: TwoPennyPublishing.com if you would
like us to consider your manuscript or book idea for publishing.

This book is dedicated to:

My wife Stephanie, for listening to these stories for decades and coming up with the idea to write them down and share them. Thank you, my love.

My four kids, Briana, Marciano IV, Mathew and Micah, for adding even more substance to not only these stories but to my life. Love you all.

My parents, Esther and Manuel, for allowing me to have these adventures while showing me all the love a Panzóncito needed. ¡Con todo mi corazon te amo!

My four sisters, brothers-in-law, nieces, nephews for all your love and for definitely adding some craziness to my life that I could write about. You are all in my heart!

The many friends I was raised with and how you all helped me raise some, uh… "Heck" as we roamed La Loma. I hope you see yourselves in here somewhere.

And to all Panzónes out there still having adventures with the best of friends… ¡Orale!

Table of Contents

1

Epi's on a Quest

I remember being called all kinds of nicknames growing up. *Mijo* was one–it's a Chicano term for all young boys. Sometimes it was "Dear" or "Sweetie" by my elementary school teachers. But the one I could never escape was *El Panzón*. If you don't get it right away, it means "chubby kid." As a 9-year-old Mexican American boy, I had a nice tan and size to me.

Okay, so I never did miss a meal, and homemade tortillas with butter always called my name back then. But you know what? Being that "well-rounded" kid (literally) never stopped me having all kinds of adventures, or from my Ma's amazing food!

My name is Epifanio—Epi, for short—or you can just call me *El Panzón*.

• • •

It was almost fall and the weather was changing. The sun was still bright but a bit of the autumn winds were blowing through. The trees were full of a combination of green and yellow leaves as times began to change. New energy was all around.

Epi had been the champion speller for Ms. Nikol's class for the past two years. Each year, he had been so close, yet so far, from winning the Great School Spelling Bee. In Mr. Clayton's class next door, there was a student who was Epi's greatest opposition to winning the spelling bee. His name was William, an African American boy similar in size to Epi and an intellectual match. Even more challenging was the fact that William seemed to always find a way to get the last word right, while Epi would consistently miss his last try.

This year would be different for Epi because he had a plan. It made him think of the Greek myths he loved to read. Maybe he was Hercules completing one of his 12 labors.[1] At least, Epi thought it was a labor trying to win against a great speller like William.

Boni arrived on her bike at the tables near Paco's Tacos. She saw Travi already there waiting for her. "¡Ay Travi!" She shook her head at him. "Here!" She threw him her hat, "but I can't stay long so don't go too far."

Today's hat was a bright, all-white hat with a wide brim, very bright and cheerful. It matched the bright pink polo shirt and skirt Boni had on. Upon receiving Boni's hat, Travi immediately

---

1   Reference to the Greek myth of "Hercules and his 12 Labors"

pulled it over his heavy head of curly hair and ran back to argue with Milo over which is a bigger event: The Super Bowl or the World Cup.

As she neared the rest of the gang, Boni rolled down her sweat pant legs from under her dress—the one her mom made her wear. She dug into her backpack and pulled out her favorite UCLA sweatshirt she got from her cousin.

She asked everyone at the tables, "Where's Epi? He wasn't at his house."

Everyone shrugged. At that moment, they all spotted Epi walking down the sidewalk from the long way around.

Normally on his bike, Epi would cut through the park on his way to Paco's. Sometimes he'd go to Big Pa's Corner Store first then across the park to get there. But today he was walking and reading. Reading wasn't unusual for Epi but reading *Webster's Dictionary* was certainly out of the ordinary.

Cuatro was out on the corner in his taco suit doing his normal job. He danced and sang his jingle, attracting passersby in their cars.

> *You wanna lots 'o tacos*
> *come to Paco's tacos*
> *You wanna some big 'o tacos*
> *come to Paco's Tacos...*

In between verses, Cuatro noticed his friend walking down the street. "Hey Epi! Whatcha doing? Did someone steal your bike?!" Before Epi could answer, Cuatro was already concluding that this must have happened, "Oh no! That's horrible!"

Of all Epi's friends, Cuatro had the biggest heart. He would always be the first to ask how you were. He would feel bad with you when times were tough, be excited with you for something good, or just be willing to help you if you needed it. Epi always liked that about him, but he could get a little too concerned at times.

Cuatro asked, "Are you sad? You're sad, huh? You can use my bike if you like. I'm working so it won't be a problem."

Epi interrupted, finally looking up from his dictionary, "No, Cuatro. I'm fine, really. I just needed to…"

With a change in demeanor, Cuatro interjects, "Oh! Your Ma told you to get out and run around again?" He nodded at Epi and turned back to sing his jingle song.

There was a reason Epi was known as *El Panzón*—he was a well-rounded, well-fed young man. He loved his Ma's flour tortillas, as much as his books and his video games. So, while his Ma loved him very much, she couldn't help reminding him occasionally to "go out and run around."

Epi gave a hrumph, and told Cuatro, "No. I am starting early this year to win the spelling bee."

After waving at the cars passing, Cuatro said, "Oh yeah. My Papí wants me to do it too with Cinco but these big words always get me." He smiled. "Besides William always wins." He saw Epi frown. "But you're always right there with him. Maybe you could win this time." Cuatro turned around quickly.

Epi walked away, nose even deeper in his dictionary. He recited a word, followed by its different definitions. He stopped, closed his eyes and spelled it slowly, "C-O-N-S-C-I-O-U-S.

Conscious." He opened his eyes and checked the page. With a big smile, he went to the next word.

In the distance, Epi noticed his little brother, Milo was chasing Travi. It would seem that during today's argument around the big games in their favorite sports, Travi must have said something about Milo's favorite players. So, here was Milo furiously chasing Travi like a linebacker in and around the tables, while Travi evaded him as if he was racing down the pitch toward a goal.

Suddenly, Travi stopped, and Milo caught up to him, nearly tackling him. As Milo put him in a headlock, Travi yelled, "Wait, wait! There's Epi." Milo turned and saw his brother walking. He let go of Travi's head. Travi fixed Boni's hat back on his mess of hair and turned to Epi and shouted, "HEY EPI!" Epi glanced up. "No bike, huh?" Epi didn't acknowledge him, "Your Ma tell you go "run around" again?"

Epi growled at him.

Milo winked at Travi. Both boys walked back over to the table to take a drink of their sodas and begin their debate again.

Cinco, Cuatro's twin brother was working in his usual spot inside the taco truck. As he wiped down the counter, he shouted out to his friend, "Hey Epi! ¿Que onda?[2] Your Ma on you again?"

Epi ignored him and kept reciting words to himself. He reached and sat on the corner of the farthest table and continued reading and reciting.

Boni walked over to the table and sat down next to Epi. "Epi, you're studying for the spelling bee already?"

_____
2   What's up? or What's happening?

"Finally," Epi said with a sigh of relief, "Yes."

Boni continued, "Your mom's on you again so you might as well, huh?"[3]

Epi yelled "¡Ya pues!" and pounded his head into the dictionary.

While everyone else was off playing a major game of Freeze Tag, Epi was still sitting at the table with his dictionary. Paco, the twins' father who owns the taco truck, brought a plate of carne asada tacos for Epi to munch on while he studied.

Paco wondered so he asked, "Epi, why aren't you out with everyone else, mijo?"[4]

Epi, not looking up from his book, replied, "This year I am going to win that spelling bee. William is not going to get the best of me again."

Paco was about to ask Epi, "…but what about having fun with friends?" but decided he was too involved in his reading.

After another plate of tacos and a lengthy time at studying, Epi looked up to see the rest of the kids walking toward him. The game ended and the sun was going down. They all knew that meant it was time to go home.

_____

3 Alright, already or enough
4 "Mijo" is a term of endearment for a boy

2

Riding Home

While each of the kids enjoyed spending time together, their individual rides home were their own solo missions, like they were each taking a different path through a huge forest. Epi once thought it was like they were Bilbo Baggins and the dwarves in THE HOBBIT.[1] They were traveling their own way through the forest.

Boni waved goodbye to the boys and rode around the block from Epi's house. As she rode, she went through her regular checklist in her mind. Did I get my hat back from Travi? Yep, I did! Sweats and t-shirt back in my bag? Check! Wearing the outfit Mom made me wear this morning? Rolling her eyes, she grumbled, "Ugh, check."

---

1   Tolkien, J.R.R. *The Hobbit*. Houghton Mifflin Harcourt, 2012. (See Appendix for reading list)

Boni truly admired her mom, Dolores. As a single mother, who worked hard as a hairdresser, she was a very caring woman; sometimes a bit too much in Boni's mind. Dolores worried about Boni being teased or bullied because of her Alopecia.

As a hairdresser, Dolores knew how important it was to have the perfect hairstyle, especially when it came to her customers. She knew her daughter did not have any. All she wanted was for Boni to be treated fairly and respectfully, as any parent would. Her idea was to raise Boni like a "little lady" who was polite and respectful, as well as smart and strong.

Dolores would buy Boni very pretty dresses and outfits with hats to match. She told Boni she needed to dress like a lady even when playing and that the hats protected her head from the sun. Dolores meant well but didn't know any other way to help her daughter. Boni tried time and time again to explain to her mom that she wasn't like that, but it didn't work. She just did what she was told.

As she rode closer to home, Boni saw her quaint house appear just around the corner. She loved her little house with its colorful flower beds planted at the front. She rode up to the house over the driveway and into the backyard where she parked her bike.

She opened the sliding door and shouted, "Hello! Mom, I'm home. I made it before it got dark. What's for dinner?"

Dolores walked in from the pantry, "Hello–" she stopped suddenly. "Bonita Esperanza! What happened to your clothes?!" She tugged at the bottom of Boni's skirt to reveal the mud splotches. "What were you doing? I thought you were just going to sit at the tables and play board games with your friends" She looked up, "And that hat!"

Boni then noticed that her brimmed, spring white hat was now drooping. She faced her mother from underneath its sagging edges. Dolores tapped her foot with her arms crossed, waiting for Boni to answer.

Boni knew she had to think quickly. She did go to the tables to play. Thinking about it more, she remembered Travi tackling her for her hat when she got to the park and then the fun of playing a long game of Freeze Tag. Those had to have been the reasons why her dress got all dirty. She couldn't tell her mom that. She also knew that Travi, with his big, bushy, hair wet from playing hard, was the reason her hat got wet; that wouldn't be good to say either.

"Uh," Boni began, still thinking, "My dress must have gotten dirty when I helped Señora Annie clean the tables." She scanned her mom's eyes to see if that worked as an excuse.

Dolores raised an eyebrow but seemed to relax a bit, then she asked Boni, "And your hat?"

"Mom, I put it on my head to protect it from the sun," said Boni. "I can't help it if my head gets sweaty from riding my bike." Boni gave a slight smile.

Dolores sighed. She let her arms down and took the hat off Boni's head.

"Ay, Boni," she smiled, "if I wash it and hang it, I think I can get it to its normal shape again. Go change. I made *arroz con pollo* [2] for dinner."

Boni gave a sigh of relief and an even bigger grin since arroz con pollo was one of her favorites.

Travi never seemed to take the same way home. If it were new, different, or just slightly dangerous, Travi would try it. His curious nature knew no bounds. His real name is Tomas. His nickname was Travi, short for Travieso, or mischief maker. His grandma, Nana Lupe, gave him that name when she noticed his nature to get into all sorts of monkey business. He could've been called Chango,[3] instead.

Today, he decided to go through the alleyway on his way home. He knew it was narrower than the streets and usually had a lot more clutter. As he was riding through, he popped a wheelie then jumped a box that had been left out behind someone's house. He was speeding up toward the end of the alley when he saw the water rushing out of Mr. Jones' backyard. Mr. Jones was steam washing his truck again, and Travi was headed straight through the suds and mud puddle nearby.

Other than the shock at suddenly being soaked and full of suds, this was the fun Travi usually liked to do. He hit his brakes suddenly and made a big splash in the mud puddle behind Mr. Jones' backyard. Travi pedaled out of the puddle from the car wash shower and back in the direction of the park. He hit his

2   A Mexican dish: Mexican rice (arroz) cooked with chunks of chicken (pollo); usually topped with cheese
3   Monkey

brakes again and turned around, heading for a return trip through the soapy waterfall.

He twisted his hand grips as if revving a motorcycle, making the motor noise with his mouth. "Vrroom! Vroom!"

He jumped on the pedals and began his trek through the "soap storm" once more. His bushy, curly hair now all drenched and fallen around his ears, Travi lifted his hands up in victory while still pedaling.

Once Travi left the alleyway, he had two more turns before he was home. While he rode, he left a messy trail of soapy mud tracks behind him. He pedaled his bike up the driveway and onto the front lawn. Travi turned on the water hose and began his evening ritual of washing down his bike and himself before he would go inside. Needless to say, whether from a soapy trail or muddy puddles on the sidewalk, Travi would need to clean up before he entered the house each day.

Through the large front window, Nana Lupe could see her little *travieso* cleaning himself up. She was always a little worried about his mischief-making, but she would never stop his curiosity. Whenever he came home, she always had a big smile on her face and waited anxiously to hear about his latest adventures. As Travi finished up his wash, Nana Lupe tapped lightly on the window and waved at him. Travi turned, full of smiles, and waved at her. He turned off the hose and walked his bike around back. He knew Nana Lupe would have dinner, and he couldn't wait to tell her about his mud bath!

Cinco and Cuatro decided to race home. They stopped at the corner and began the countdown. "3-2-1…Go!"

They were off! Cinco took the lead. Then it was Cuatro! It was a tie, so the last stretch home would determine who won! Suddenly, Cuatro turned off into the Wilsons' yard, a neighbor who lived a few houses down from the boys. Meanwhile, Cinco knew he was winning and turned to tell Cuatro he lost. He swung his head around and noticed his brother wasn't racing anymore. He scanned the street and saw Cuatro a few houses down kneeling near a little boy. He rolled his eyes and slowed down. When he stopped, he called back to Cuatro, but he didn't get a response. Cinco got back on his pedals and rode to where Cuatro had stopped.

"Who are you saving now?" asked Cinco, who saw little Greg Wilson on the ground crying.

"Cinco, don't be mean," said Cuatro, reprimanding his brother, "Can't you see Greg fell down?"

It was apparent that their neighbor, Greg Wilson, a boy younger than the twins, had fallen. He was wearing a helmet and was holding what appeared to be the handlebars from a pedal scooter. Cinco wondered to himself, "Where is the rest of it?" He looked up the long uphill driveway the Wilsons had and noticed where the rest of the contraption was.

Cuatro tended to Greg like a field nurse, and asked "Are you okay? Oh! You skinned your knee, but it doesn't look too bad." Cuatro took his water bottle and his towel off his own bike. He then poured some water over Greg's cut knee. While he dabbed the knee dry, he said, "Later on, ask your mom for some Neo-fix-it stuff to put on it and a bandage."

Greg nodded and sniffled a bit.

"What happened to your scooter?"

"I don't know." He sniffled again. "I just got it, and my dad said he would put it together tomorrow on his day off. I couldn't wait, so I put it together myself up there in the garage. I put my helmet on and started to ride it down. I was getting ready to turn onto the grass when it all started to come apart. I just fell off the side and slid on the cement." He started to cry again. "Now look at it! It's broken and my dad is going to be mad because I didn't wait for him." Greg's sob grew louder.

Cuatro winced a bit from his loud cry but kept patting him on the shoulder. Cinco covered his ears and sighed.

"Let me take a look at it." offered Cinco, as he gathered up the pieces.

Cuatro smiled big. He knew if anyone could fix it, it was his brother.

Cinco took out his pocket kit with all his little tools attached. He never went anywhere without it. He walked up the hill, picking up the pieces on his way to the Wilsons' garage. He took a quick glance at the directions then began reassembling the scooter. When he was close to finishing, he noticed the handlebars wouldn't stay attached. He got up and searched for a piece he might have missed around the driveway. With no luck, he returned to the garage. He ran his hand through the box and found what he was looking for: a lock pin that holds the handlebars on. He put it in place, giving each bolt and screw a tight twist, and then met Cuatro and Greg outside.

"Here you go," said Cinco. "You missed a piece that held on the handlebars. Next time, either read all the directions or wait for your dad, okay?"

Greg nodded.

Cinco patted him on the head and grabbed Cuatro. "I'm still racing you home."

Cuatro just smiled at his brother.

Milo and Epi were the last to leave Paco's Tacos that day, mainly because of football.

As the gang all sped off for home that night, two boys from their school, Billy and John, rode by on their way home as well. Now Billy was a Giants fan. Milo was an Eagles fan. When it came to professional football, there was no love lost between these two teams. The same can be said of their fans. Today, Billy challenged Milo and Epi to a quick 2-on-2 game, but Epi and Milo declined.

"Maybe next time. We have to get home," said Milo. He was getting on the back of his bike so his brother could ride it as well.

"Yeah, fly home Eagles," scoffed Billy as he adjusted his backwards baseball cap to accommodate his long hair. "The Giants are stomping through."

John, the smaller of the two, joined Billy by stomping around Epi and Milo. Milo stopped and looked at his brother.

Epi shook his head. "We need to get home. You know what Ma says about staying out late."

Milo nodded and turned to Billy again to tell him, "No," when he saw him and John doing what looked like the chicken dance as they spelled out Eagles. Spelling out Eagles was a *serious* fan song.

Even more annoyed, Milo spun around to Epi. Milo's little face expressed both shock and irritation at what he saw. He pointed at the boys as they mocked their team. Epi, with a smirk on his face, slowly got off the bike and looked at his little brother.

"Let's do this!"

The boys went out to the open grassy area of Hamilton Park to set up the game. They decided they would play 2-hand touch, not tackle football. The far two trees would be Milo's and Epi's end zone. The garbage cans on the other side would be Billy's and John's. Epi suggested a short game since it was getting late. They all agreed the first team to three touchdowns won.

"We call 'winner's' ball," said Milo.

They shook on it and ran to their spots at the opposite ends of the field. "Winner's" meant the team who scored would receive the kickoff immediately after. It usually made for a quicker game.

Epi and Milo would receive first since Billy and John made the challenge. Epi and Milo got into their two-man huddle, whispered their game plan, and then yelled "break" as they clapped their hands. They were ready.

Billy threw the ball as a "kickoff" as usual, and Epi caught it just beyond midfield. He tossed it back to Milo and ran up the field, ready to block. He first came in contact with Billy, who closely matched Epi's height but not his girth. With a rough shoulder block, Billy was out of the way soon enough. Milo followed his brother. Next, Epi had to meet John. John was smaller and quicker than Billy. Milo knew what to do and shadowed his big brother closely. When John tried to run around Epi, Milo slipped out the other way and turned on the speed, racing down the length of the field. Billy, who had recovered from the block, was chasing him down but didn't get close. Milo scored, did his first of what he planned to be many touchdown dances, and gave the ball to Epi to "kickoff."

The next touchdown for the brothers came off a deflected pass from Billy to John. For this game, you were not allowed to rush into the quarterback until you counted to 5, slowly; usually 1-alligator, 2-alligator, 3-alligator and so on.

Epi counted, "Five!" then rushed in toward Billy.

Billy couldn't get away and tried to pass the ball. Epi put his hand up and made a jump—not the highest, but it worked. His fingers tipped the football, and it fell right into his hands. He tucked it under his arm and ran for the end zone. Epi was not the fastest, but he was always focused. For speed, you needed Milo.

As soon as he saw the tipped ball fall into his brother's hands, Milo zoomed in to help. When it seemed that Billy and John would catch Epi, Milo crossed right in front of both, long enough for Epi to make it over the goal line. Touchdown!

Of course, no matter how much fun the boys were having, they both knew it was getting late, and they had to get home. Billy and John had just scored, and the game was going longer than expected. Epi was losing energy. He loved the game, but it was tiring. The brothers knew if they got one more touchdown for themselves, they would win. They decided to speed up their game, no matter how tired they were. Milo and Epi lined up. Epi was quarterback, as usual, and Milo would run out for the pass.

"Hike!" yelled Epi, and Milo snapped the ball to him.

Epi stepped back while Milo sprinted up the field, faked left with one step, then turned his head right to see the pass. Epi had already thrown the ball, and Milo caught it in two steps. He raced another ten yards before John tagged him. First Down.

They set up again the same way–Epi as quarterback and Milo as receiver.

"Hike!"

This play was a fake pass. Milo sprinted down the sidelines. Billy counted, "5-alligator!" and ran in for Epi.

Epi dodged Billy and took two steps forward before heaving the ball as hard as he could. The ball sailed high and far. Milo was sprinting down field with John more than three steps behind him. Milo turned his head over his left shoulder and caught the ball as he crossed the goal line. It was a touchdown! Epi and Milo had won!

Milo didn't do his usual touchdown dance, and instead he slammed the ball on the ground and pointed at his big brother. Epi pointed back at Milo in celebration. He then turned to Billy and John to give them each a high-five.

"Good game," Epi told them.

He ran toward Milo, who was already at the bikes. He jumped on his bike and gave a double high-five to his little brother.

"Thanks for playing, Epi." said Milo, and honor to their favorite team had been restored.

"Whatever, Milo," Epi smiled back. "I got you. Let's go now. You know it's getting dark!"

They sped off for home. They were tired and sweaty but victorious.

Epi knew there weren't many times he could be called "Speedy," whether on a bike or on foot. However, when it was dinner time and Ma was cooking, everyone knew to watch out! El Panzón got his name because he *loved* his Ma's food.

The boys rode quickly after the game—Milo on the seat, Epi feverishly pedaling. They rocketed up the steep driveway and to the side of their house, where they greeted their dog, Tesoro. The name meant "treasure," which he was, most of the time, except when the boys forget to clean up after him.

Epi jumped of the bike and entered the house. Milo stood it up near the gate to the backyard and followed Epi through the back door. They didn't know any better than to use the back door for everything. This was how everyone was expected to enter. In fact, they couldn't remember the last time they had used the front door. They rushed in and found their Ma in the kitchen, as usual, since it was dinner time.

"Milo! Panzón! You were almost late," scolded Ma. "¡Tu sabes![4] You-Know-Who could have gotten you."

Epi's home was filled with two languages: Spanish and English. It was an amazing combination of culture and communication. Epi's parents taught their children to proudly express themselves in both. Ma and Pop showed that by sharing a mixture of both languages at the same time. They seamlessly wove Spanish and English into every conversation…especially Ma when she got excited!

---

4   You know

The boys nodded in agreement at their mother's scolding, while still huffing and puffing from the football game and ride.

Ma continued, "¡Ya, vallanse!⁵ Go get cleaned up. Your Pop should be home soon."

"Yes, Ma," came from both boys as they raced from the kitchen.

Epi passed the table and saw what their sister Paola had in her hands. He winked at Milo and tapped her on one shoulder, which made her turn. With Paola distracted, Milo grabbed a flour tortilla from the plate in her hands. He split it in half and gave a piece to Epi as they escaped. They heard Paola complain to Ma about it.

Ma, halfheartedly, shouted "Ay Panzón, Milo, don't do that to your sister!"

But the boys could see a slight smile on her face. Paola gave a harrumph and went back to setting the table.

The boys went into the bathroom to wash up. They looked in the mirror and gave their hair a quick comb. They knew either Paola or Ma would tell them something if they didn't. They went to their room and changed their t-shirts since they had become wet from swimming and sweaty from the football game.

By the time Milo chose which of his Eagles t-shirts to put on, they could hear Pop's truck drive up and park. They ran to the back door as he opened it. They both greeted him with either a high-five or a knuckle punch, and each boy took to his nightly ritual. Milo grabbed Pop's work shirt and lunch box while Epi helped Pop take off his heavy work boots.

---

5   Go along

The boys knew their Pop worked hard every day, and they felt this was how they could help him relax when he got home. Neither Mom nor Pop ever asked the boys to do this. It was just something Epi started when he was younger. He was happy to see his Pop home. Milo joined when he was old enough. Every day, Pop would tell the boys he was happy to see them and very often he would tell them they didn't have to do all this. They would smile up at him, and he knew they would do it tomorrow anyway. He was proud of them for it.

After the boys welcomed him home, Pop entered the kitchen and said, "Hi," to his "Hon." Paola told the boys it was short for "Honey," but they couldn't remember him ever calling Ma that. Paola gave him a hug and a kiss on the cheek. After being greeted with all this love, Pop washed up. Now, they were ready for dinner.

It didn't matter to Epi what was for dinner. He knew it was going to be good. He didn't have a favorite dish from his mom's daily menu. Everything she made was his favorite, although he really did enjoy when she made enchiladas.

They all sat down at the table together, said a blessing over the food, and began to eat. Ma never seemed to sit down for very long. She would be up, tending to the family, more than eating her own food. Even when Pop asked her to sit with him, she would only do so for a little while before getting up to get something or to flip a tortilla that was on the *placa*.[6] Paola and Epi came to the decision they would take turns getting up quickly to serve seconds or get Pop something, once Ma finally

---

6   A flat grill for cooking tortillas, pancakes, etc.; a griddle

sat down. She'd slightly frown, but Pop would smile and wink at us.

Dinner time was much the same every night. Pop and Ma would listen to the latest adventures from each of their children: Milo's touchdowns, Epi's books, and Paola's school events and fun at her part-time job at the movie theater. Ma would share what she had done and at times what she had heard from her *comadres*.[7] As everyone sat back full, except Epi who usually asked for another helping, Pop would share stories from work and from his day's newspaper. No one would dare to ask to be excused until he had finished. Epi didn't want to leave anyhow but he could see his sister and little brother sometimes getting antsy.

When dinner was over, each of the three kids had a chore: the boys would wipe off the plates into the trash can, as well as clear the table. Epi swept and Milo fed Tesoro. Ma and Paola wiped down the counters and washed the dishes. While the kitchen was getting cleaned up, Pop would check with Ma if there was anything that needed fixing or if the car needed a tune up. If so, he'd get right to it. When they were done with their after-dinner tasks, Epi and Milo would help him. The boys weren't allowed to help for long if they had homework. If there was nothing that needed fixing, Pop would sit and help Paola, Milo and Epi with their homework.

Whether Pop had anything to repair or not, once dinner was complete, he would turn up the music Ma had playing. There was always music in the house. When a "good" song came on Pop would pull Ma to him and the kitchen became a dance floor.

---

7   Close female friends

Paola knew she wouldn't get Ma back to help but she smiled at them anyway. Milo would mimic them dancing using a towel or something as a dance partner. Epi would get in between them as he swept the floor, teasing them, until one of them would nudge him out of the way.

When it came to bedtime, it was almost always a chore to get Milo to go to sleep. Epi's thought was that his brother must have one of those batteries, from the commercials, that never stopped. It was usually by the third time he was told to go to sleep that he would. The first was by Paola who would bang on the wall next door. Next, it was Ma shouting from their bedroom. Finally, Pop's deep voice would say "Emiliano," and Milo would stop.

After a fun day like today, Epi, from the top bunk, was very ready for sleep. He nestled into his pillow, said goodnight to everyone, and pulled his blankets up.

"Hey Epi!" asked Milo, from his snug bottom bunk.

Epi grunted at his brother, not wanting to move out of his warm cocoon.

Milo continued, "Did you hear that Cinco said he was going to build a bike ramp at his house this weekend? Travi asked him to be the first to try it."

Epi rolled over and faced the wall with his pillow over his ears. It didn't work. He could still hear Milo.

Milo continued, "Cuatro and Boni are going to look for pillows since they thought Travi might need them if he was going first. And, you know what else? I hope Billy and John want a rematch." Epi's little brother's ability to fight falling asleep at bedtime was in high gear this night.

Now fully awake from his brother's continued jabbering on, Epi took his pillow off his head and sat up. He answered, "If you're going to keep on talking, I am going to need some more food for energy to stay awake." He kicked off his blankets and turned his feet over the edge of his bed.

Mid-sentence, Milo stopped and asked Epi, "Where are you going?" as he saw his brother slide down the side of their bunk bed to the floor.

"Shhhh." Epi shushed his brother, "I am going to the kitchen. Ma left some tortillas in the basket." He tiptoed off.

Epi quietly opened the door and headed down the hallway. Milo scratched his head, shrugged his shoulders, and rolled himself into his blankets. He figured he'd finish his story when Epi got back.

After about 3 minutes of waiting, which is felt like forever to Milo, he thought to himself, "Actually, Ma's tortillas right now are not a bad idea." He jumped out of bed and tiptoed down the hallway to join his big brother.

At the dinner table, the boys both gorged themselves on Ma's fresh flour tortillas with a little butter. Epi poured some orange juice for both to wash it all down. After half the basket was emptied, the well-contented brothers walked quietly back to bed. Quietly, and a little slower for their feast. The boys were full, satisfied, and ready to sleep, even Milo. He figured he'd save the rest of his stories for tomorrow night.

Epi relaxed in his bed. He pulled his blankets up and sleepily, after today's adventures, he half expected to see furry Hobbit feet pop out of the bottom.

3

Now I Know!

On Saturday, after the cartoons were watched and the Frooty Rooty cereal was eaten, what came next? CHORES.

In Epi's home, all three kids had "work" to do. Everyone had to clean their rooms and change the sheets on their beds. Paola had the bathrooms to clean and helped Ma hang the laundry and clean the kitchen. Milo swept and cleaned the carport and patio. Epi had the backyard to clean and mow, plus both he and Milo would help Pop with the front lawn. It's not like the kids were ever excited to do chores, but they knew there was no getting around it.

Today, however, Epi was anxious to get all his chores done quickly. Ronny, from his Scout troop, had asked him to sleepover. Between school, scouts, and his constant pursuit of spelling prowess, a sleepover at Ronny's would be a nice mini-vacation.

Ma, as she always did, told Epi he could go, but ONLY if he finished everything to her satisfaction. The trouble was Ma's standards were super high. Army sergeants could learn something from her.

Epi said "Ok, Ma I did my work. I threw the trash away. I fixed my bed. I put my clothes away. I smashed the cans. I even picked up Tesoro's *caquitas*." [1] Tesoro[2] was a mixed breed, and Epi wasn't actually sure what he was mixed with. Tesoro howled like a hound, jumped around like a Chihuahua, and was slender like a greyhound. Regardless of his pedigree, Tesoro was the most loyal of any dog.

Epi finally got to his question with Ma, "Can I go to Ronny's now?"

Ronny was one of Epi's friends from school and his mom, Sarah, was the Pack Leader for their Scout troop. His dad, Doug, was a truck driver and always brought Ronny back some very cool souvenirs. The coolest thing about staying over at Ronny's house was Epi knew that Ronny's mom let him stay up late. That meant the boys could play video games and watch TV all night. That's a great weekend! His mom also let Ronny eat all kinds of junk food: chips, soda, snack cakes, whatever. He said it was because he was so skinny. She said he needed to eat.

Ronny was a tall boy—taller than Epi—and stick skinny, especially compared to Epi's large frame. Still, Epi never ate as much as Ronny did and he always gained weight.

_____

1 Dog "droppings"
2 Treasure

Epi thought, "Must be what Ms. Nikols' science lesson in school meant the other day: everyone has a different metabolism." He didn't quite understand what that meant, but it sounded "scientific" enough for him.

Mom gave Epi a stern look, "Ay, mijo. Let me see first." She would need to do a thorough inspection before she would let Epi go anywhere.

She walked into the kitchen from the living room. The first thing she inspected was the large kitchen trash can. "Ay Epi. Haven't I told you what to do when you throw out the kitchen trash bag? Afterwards you use one of the paper grocery bags as a trash bag. Put an egg carton at the bottom for leaks and fold the edges of the bag so it's easier to pull out?" She shook her head at him.

Epi acknowledged her reprimand but secretly rolled his eyes. He knew Ma and Pop had a system for everything and he knew he simply had to remember them all.

Mom further reprimanded Epi, "*Te digo*,[3] if you can't remember how to do that, how will you remember when to come home?"

Every small failure could be a statement of Epi's ability to survive life. Epi quickly went to the storage closet, grabbed the egg carton, and placed it at the bottom of the bag. He looked up at Ma and said, "Ma, NOW can I go? You said when I finished, I could go and stay at Ronny's tonight."

---

3   I tell you

Ma finally relinquished, "Okay, *ya ahora puedes ir*[4] but be back by dinner tomorrow. Call me when you get there too."

"Ok, Ma, I will call when I get there." Epi grabbed his duffle bag, which was already packed, and was on his bike in a flash.

Epi loved his bike—a Murray Cat series bicycle. Like his Pop, Epi was forever tinkering, especially on his bike. He painted it, changed rims, the handlebars, etc.—always trying to make it faster. As he jumped on it now, he headed up the street, passing neighbors and familiar spots. Ronny lived on the other side of the freeway passed their school. Epi was so excited that he popped a couple of wheelies and made small jumps off the curb. It was a fun ride. As he rode, however, he knew what was coming. When he made the last turn, he saw it: THE BRIDGE.

"Okay, this time I can make it!" Epi said to himself.

The Bridge was a pedestrian bridge that took neighborhood kids over the freeway to all the fun spots on the other side. While Epi's home and many of his friends' homes were on this side of the freeway, everything else Epi needed for entertainment was on the other side. It was all located in or near The City Heights Shopping Center—The Big Fat Donut Shop, the bookshop Gotta Read, and Save-Much Mart with its own batch of video games. It helped Epi kill time when his mom was grocery shopping. Of course, his school, Hillside Elementary, was also on that side of the freeway as well as today's destination: Ronny's house.

The slope side of The Bridge was always fun—going down fast and slamming your brakes as you got to the end. However,

---

4   Now you can go

the challenge was taking the upside without having to stop and walk. So far Epi had not been able to do it.

Epi began to pedal his bike as hard as he could. "This time I'm starting earlier. I am breathing right and (he paused) here... we... go!"

Epi sped up the ramp. He was making good progress, only to slow down midway, breathing hard then finally stopped.

Epi, panted heavily, "I... was... almost... there." He got off his bike, and with a second wind, he began walking his bike up the rest of the way. Epi reached the top and took another slightly longer break before he started again.

Now smiling, Epi got back on his bike. He knew the other side of the bridge was the most fun.

"Here we go!!!"

Epi sped across to the slope side. After reaching the desired speed, he coasted his bike down the ramp. Suddenly Epi SLAMMED on the brakes halfway down, leaving a black strip behind him. Epi yelled like a wild man with a huge grin. This was the payoff every time he rode his bike this way. Stopping at the bottom after a great slide always made The Bridge worth it!

After a quick stop at The Big Fat Donut Shop for a water and a big fat donut, Epi arrived at Ronny's house and knocked on the door.

Ronny answered and greeted Epi, "What's up? Come on in. You staying the night, right?"

"Yeah," he told his friend, "I finally got my mom to let me come over." They high-fived each other. They both knew they were in for a great time!

Epi and Ronny went into the living room. He greeted Ronny's mother, Sarah, who was behind their TV.

"Hello, Mrs. Sarah. Thank you for letting me come over." Epi scanned the room. He had never been to Ronny's house. It was very nice and very big. He wondered, "How many people lived here?" then he remembered it was just Ronny, his sister, Julie, and Ronny's parents. He had been reading a book recently—<u>The House on Mango Street</u>[5]—where the author had described all the different people in her neighborhood. That they were all different in their own ways. This felt like that. "Something new," I think.

Ronny's dad, Doug, was away for work on long-distance runs, so, Ronny, his little sister, Julie, and his mom took care of the house. Sarah was very handy with a set of tools. Right now, she was setting up the new TV Doug had purchased on his last stop home.

Sarah looked up from behind the entertainment center, and returned Epi's greeting, "Hello Little Epi. You are always welcome in our home."

Epi liked it when she called him "little." Not many people could call Epi, "little." He thought if anyone could, they could. Sarah and Doug were both at least 6' tall and "strongly built," Epi thought. When he first met them, he thought they were giants.

The boys spent the day playing. First, outside—a little bit of hoops, some football as if they were in Super Bowl, and of course riding bikes around the block. After eating pizza for dinner, the boys watched a video: "The Man With 3 Heads." It was just scary

---

5   Cisneros, Sandra. *The House on Mango Street.* Arte Público Press, 1984.

enough for the boys to keep the lights on but not so much that they turned the movie off.

The rest of the night was even better. Ronny had a TV in his room, which was amazing to Epi. Ronny also had a brand-new video game set in there and all the latest games. First, some racing carts then the new boxing game. The night ended, with some Space Invasion action, mainly because Mrs. Sarah finally yelled at Ronny for them both to go to sleep. The boys ended up falling asleep on the carpet in Ronny's room still holding the game controllers.

After a long night of junk food and video games, the boys slept in late. Mrs. Sarah shouted to them, "Boys! Get up now, lazy bones. I've got lunch."

"It's LUNCHTIME!" Epi thought.

Suddenly opening his eyes, he sprung out of bed. You can be certain Epi did not miss meals. He knew he had already slept past breakfast, so lunch was crucial. Epi and Ronny walked into the dining room area where Ronny's mom was setting the table.

Epi's eyes opened wide as he saw the table setting. "Wow! Matching stuff: plates, forks, chairs. That was so weird. We all have different forks and favorite plates."

In Ma and Pop's life together, they had collected a variety of silverware sets and plate combinations. Of course, having 3 kids and so many nieces and nephews who might break something here and there, plus Ma offering leftovers to all who visit, their home had an eclectic assortment of tableware. At Epi's house, it was a ritual for each of the family members to seek out their favorite plate, fork, or cup.

Epi thought to himself "I'm starving. Maybe we will have hamburgers. No, I didn't smell the grease. Maybe bologna sandwiches. Yeah...mmmmmmm."

Ronny's mom placed chips and a pitcher of Kool-Aid on the table with cloth napkins.

Epi asked, "Ronny, why do I have a towel? Did you run out of paper towels?"

Ronny replied, "No, Epi. Why?""

Epi a little confused, "I have a washcloth here. Where's the paper towels or napkins?"

Ronny laughed. "Those *are* the napkins."

Epi thought to himself, "Okay but you're going to have to wash these."

Sarah said to the boys, "Okay, here we go. Hope you're hungry."

She placed the largest, yellowest, gooiest thing he had ever seen on Epi's plate. Epi had been taught to respect adults and eat what you're offered as a guest. Nevertheless, the item quivering on his plate made following that rule very difficult. To him, this thing was... WEIRD.

He thought to himself, "Gross! What was that?"

Ronny smiled big at his mom, "Thanks, Mom. I am famished." Ronny tucked right into his lunch.

Sarah said, "I knew it was your favorite. Mine too." She jumped right into eating, as well.

"What do I do?" thought Epi, "This jelly thing was moving but they are eating it like nothing."

He saw Ronny take another huge bite of his lunch. Epi's stomach grumbled a bit, "Plus I am so hungry." He opened his bag of chips and ate them quickly, but it didn't help much. He was still hungry. He drank his glass of Kool-Aid, plus more, and still, his tummy was rumbling. Epi worried, "I have to eat something, or I'll starve to death, plus I don't want to be rude."

He saw Ronny and his mom grab the "thing" with their hands, so he tried as well. It just felt too squishy; he just couldn't do it.

Feeling like lunch was almost over, Epi came up with a plan. He quickly and with much disgust grabbed the thing on his plate, ripped off a huge piece and placed it into a spare paper napkin Mrs. Sarah had placed on the table. He then stuffed it all into his pocket.

Much like at school when you must finish everything before the Lunch Ladies let you leave the cafeteria, Epi waited for Ronny's mom to excuse them to go play. Once excused, he rushed to his duffle bag and placed the thing in it. He didn't want to just throw it in the trash can for fear of Ronny or his mom seeing it.

After lunch, the boys watched TV for a while, but Epi was worried about the stuff still sitting in his bag. After a while, Epi couldn't take it anymore. He said to Ronny, "I gotta go. My mom wanted me to help her before dinner."

Ronny puzzled, "You sure?"

"Yeah, man. I'll see you at school Monday. Bye, Mrs. Sarah." Epi grabbed his duffle bag and headed out the door.

Quick as a shot, Epi was on his bike and raced down the street. He felt a little bad for leaving so suddenly but knew he just had to.

The next obstacle was of course The Bridge. It lay between Ronny's and Epi's houses but when Epi was hungry—EPI WAS HUNGRY! He said to himself, "Forget this!" dug in and pedaled as hard as he could.

For the first time since learning to ride to school, Epi took the upside of The Bridge without stopping; he crossed the top and down the other side with barely any brakes.

Epi raced home the rest of the way, through the streets, up his driveway and through his back door in record time.

Ma, shocked at his entrance, nearly screamed at him, "¿¡Panzón ?!"

Without answering Ma, Epi went straight for her warm stack of flour tortillas that she always kept near the stove. He threw one on the *comal*,[6] got the butter and made the first of three butter tortillas in a row. When he was done, he was calmer and ultimately satisfied.

Ma and Paola stood there amazed and a little frightened.

Ma asked Epi, with concern, "¿¡Mijo?! ¡¿*Que te paso*?!*[7] They didn't feed you or que?!"

Epi answered, "Ma! (in between munching) Now! (munch) Now I know (munch) why Ronny (Munch) was so skinny." He swallowed his last bite. "And his mom, too."

---

6   Flat griddle used on the stove for cooking/ warming tortillas
7   What happened to you?

Not understanding any of this, Ma asked him, "What are you talking about, Panzón? "

Epi stated with the utmost certainty, "Ronny was skinny because his mom doesn't know how to cook! That's why!"

Mom shook her head, "What do you mean she doesn't know how to cook?"

His older sister, Paola, finally jumped in, having witnessed the scene. She interjected, "She brings stuff to your class potlucks and the kids eat it. What are you talking about?"

Epi rebutted his sister, "She always brings chips, or something bought at the store."

His Ma and sister gave him a smirk in disbelief.

"I'm serious," he continued, "Poor Ronny gets fed cold...uh... cold yellow goop."

Ma gave him a look, "I don't understand."

Finally, Epi went to his duffle bag near the back door. He pulled out the gunk still wrapped in the napkin and put it on the table. Ma and Paola looked at the item, looked at each other, then began laughing.

"Why are you laughing?! I was starving," exclaimed Epi.

Ma said "That's part of an Egg Salad Sandwich. My worker friend, Mrs. Jones, used to bring it to work for lunch. See? The bread? The white for the boiled egg? It's like deviled eggs your Tia[8] makes, but in a bread."

Epi scrunched his face. He said "Deviled eggs in a bread?! ¡Orale! That's gross."

---

8   Aunt

Paola added, "No it's not. My friend Jenny brings that to work for a lunch break at the movie theater. I tried it. It's not bad."

Epi gawked at his sister, "Really?"

As Epi contemplated it all, he sat down at the kitchen table eating his fourth or fifth tortilla. He thought about how Ronny and his mom enjoyed their lunch. "They liked it, I guess," he wondered, "And how did I not know about this. Ma and Paola knew."

In the end, he came to his own conclusion. He decided to share it with his Ma and his sister, "All I am saying was I figure everyone likes what they like and that's okay, but next time I go over to Ronny's house, I'm taking some tortillas."

He put another tortilla to warm. Flipping it over, he suddenly realized the streets around Ronny's house were named for fruit and his was Mango Street!

4

Ice Cream Dash

One unique aspect of Epi's neighborhood was the weather. It was always a hot summer that led to a warm few months in the fall. One perk from this climate was that summertime treat-giver stayed around a little longer: the Ice Cream Man and his white delivery van, with a large sliding window on the passenger side, decorated with stickers advertising the wide variety of ice cream offered. On the top of the vehicle was a plastic figure in the shape of a smiling ice cream cone, along with the most important piece to the truck's advertising: The Speaker! The kids all knew it was Ice Cream Truck time when they heard the music that was a combination of "Happy Birthday," "Pop Goes the Weasel," and "Jingle Bells." The Ice Cream Man always had all their favorites: Fudge Sticks, GIANT Icicles, even scooped ice cream in cups. Epi's favorite was double-thick ice cream sandwiches! Those always made the warm start-of-school weather more bearable. However, there were some times Epi didn't always catch the truck.

This particular school day was quickly becoming a scorcher. After school, Boni and Travi were at Paco's Tacos already, trying to stay cool under the umbrellas at the tables.

As she wiped her head with her *paño*,[1] Boni declared, "It is so hot today. I'm so glad I brought water." She took her water jug off her bike and took a cool, soothing drink from it.

Travi gave her a longing look. She smiled and handed the jug to him.

Cinco was behind the counter inside the truck. "How hot do you think I feel?!" He wiped his forehead with his towel, "and Cuatro's out there in the Taco Suit!" He pointed out toward the street corner at his brother.

After hearing his brother's comments about the heat, Cuatro turned, his face drenched. He smiled and said, "It's not so bad." A passing car honked approval for his dancing.

Cinco jabbed back, "'*Not -So -bad*'? *Then -why -are -you -sweating -so -much*?" Cinco's voice sounded funny because he had his face directly in the path of the fan sitting on the counter next to him.

Cuatro lifted his official Paco's Tacos hat he was wearing to reveal a shower cap full of ice. "See?" He put the hat back on and did a double wave at a large delivery truck as it sped by. The driver waved back at him.

---

1 Bandana

Cinco just rolled his eyes, but knew his brother had the right idea. Boni and Travi smiled, seemingly thinking the same thing: A bag full of ice on their heads would feel great!

There was no denying the sun was at work on this hot summer day. So much that Boni actually kept her hat for herself today. Usually, she would immediately pass it to Travi, but today was too hot and sunny for her clear, bald head to be without cover.

Epi and his little brother, Milo, were walking toward Paco's Tacos and the rest of the gang from the other side of the park. Milo, as anxious and energetic as always, was growing frustrated.

"It is HOT! And why are we walking anyway?" he asked Epi.

Epi turned to Milo and explained, "Pop took my bike to his work to fix the handlebars, remember?"

Milo nodded but asked again, "Ok, then why am I walking? My bike works. It's soooo hot!"

Epi gave his brother that look of annoyance and reminded him further, "Ma said since I wasn't riding and had to walk, you could, too."

Milo rolled his eyes at his big brother, but he knew he was right. Besides, there was no arguing with Ma.

Halfway through the park and within sight of the gang, Epi and Milo heard one of the best sounds of the summer: The Ice Cream Truck music! Both boys began to run. The only problem was Milo was much faster than his brother. Epi was known as *El Panzón* for a good reason. As Pop put it lovingly, "Mijo, you're big." To Epi being big had its advantages, for example, being picked first for football at recess. However, being speedy wasn't one of them.

Epi was moving, to be sure, but not enough to catch the Ice Cream man. Milo knew this. He turned back toward his brother who was losing distance with each step.

"Do you want me to buy one for you?" He yelled back at Epi, "I have money."

Maybe as a mixture of pride and embarrassment, he told Milo, "No, I'll get there. You go ahead."

Milo reluctantly agreed and ran faster toward the tables and the rest of the gang.

Milo arrived and stood in line behind Cinco who was next to get his treat. As soon as Milo got his, he told the Ice Cream Man that his brother was coming. Milo looked back and saw Epi had begun walking instead. He waved his hand at Epi to hurry. Epi waved back, but without the confidence that he would make it in time.

From his position, Epi could see Milo at the window then heard the music start again—this meant the Ice Cream Truck was preparing to leave. Epi began to run again but after a few steps, he saw the truck drive off. He walked the rest of the way.

When he arrived, everyone was eating their ice cream. Travi loved his Fudge Sticks, which he always made a mess of. Boni consistently bought the GIANT Icicles, while Cuatro and Cinco always purchased snow cones, Cuatro with his Lime green and Cinco with his Bubblegum blue. Epi knew Milo would've gotten a scoop of vanilla ice cream w/ gummy worms all mixed in.

Everyone greeted him between bites and licks of their ice cream favorites. They were so enjoying their treats they hardly noticed when Epi said "Hi," and sat down at the far end of their table. He sat there thinking about the ice cream sandwich he wished he had.

Cuatro was the first to notice his friend sitting away from the group. He walked over. "Hey, Epi." He noticed Epi's sad face, "Awwww, you didn't get one? That's a bummer." Cuatro's face always showed his emotions. Right now, he felt bad for his friend, "Here Epi, you can have the rest of mine." He stretched his hand out to him.

"It's Ok, Cuatro, I'm fine," replied Epi.

"No, really," insisted Cuatro.

Epi not wanting to take his friend's ice cream, but also, not wanting to hurt his feelings, "Thanks Cuatro, but, uh, I, uh, am allergic to lime." Epi gave a slight smile, and Cuatro responded, "Oh, ok." and he walked back to his brother, Cinco.

At that point, Milo walked over, looking for his brother, "Epi! Where are you?" Setting his eyes at the far end of the table, "Hey, I was looking for you."

"Yeah, I knew I would get here after the Ice Cream Truck left, so I came in behind the taco truck," Epi sniffled.

"Don't be so sad, Epi. The Ice Cream Man was in a hurry," he said. Milo took his hands from behind his back, "Here."

Epi looked up and saw Milo handing him a jumbo ice cream sandwich. "I know you said not to, but I did anyway."

Epi's smile was wider than normal, "Thanks Milo."

After that day, Epi's thoughts were filled with the question: "How do I make myself faster like Hermes, the messenger of the gods in his Greek myths book?!" [2] He watched professional and college football on TV with Milo and saw how big those guys were. He thought if those humongous players could be fast like that, he could too.

His first idea was athletic training. What that meant, he had no idea. He needed to ask his older sister, Paola. She ran track on the high school team. Her team had already started their workouts to prepare for the spring season so Epi believed she would definitely know how to train. He went to her room to ask.

Epi walked down the hall to his sister's room. He could hear her music playing through the door. He knew he would be bothering her, but he was determined to solve his problem.

He knocked on Paola's bedroom door. "Pao-Pao," he called her.

She growled at him, "Don't call me that. Go away." She went back to listening to her favorite music. Paola, like most big sisters, was not always open to listening to her little brothers.

"No, no, I'm sorry, Paola," apologized Epi. "Seriously, I have a question to ask you." He knocked again, "Please let me in."

She stopped her music and went to the door. "What, Epi?" as she opened it to find her brother there with a serious look on his face. "You OK?"

---

2   D'Aulaire, Ingri; D'Aulaire, Edgar Parin. *D'Aulaires' Book of Greek Myths*. Delacorte Press, 1992.

"I'm OK, but I wanted to ask you: how did you get to be so fast? I've seen you run your races at the track meet, and you have super speed," he told her.

With a confused smile Paola said, "Uh, thanks."

"How did you get that way?" he asked, as if doing research.

She stood there in her doorway with her arms crossed and just stared at her brother. The look in his eyes made her believe he was serious about his question.

She answered, "Well, for the track team, I have to go to practice every day. The coach plans different drills for us to do, depending on what event we are in. I am a sprinter, so he usually starts us out running together for warm up. Next, we do short sprints and long sprints. If it's close to a meet, we will do our actual event and he will time us to show us how we are doing."

She noticed Epi had taken out a small notepad. "Why are you so interested? It's early in the school year so this can't be a school project?"

Epi didn't feel like telling her the real reason—that he wanted to get fast enough to catch the Ice Cream Man. He told her, "I am trying to finally beat Cuatro in a race."

Paola squinted her eyes as if she didn't believe him.

He went on, "How does a running workout start?"

Paola decided to humor him, "The first thing we do every practice is stretch." She showed him a few: toe touches for the back of his legs, calf stretches, leg pulls for the front of his legs. Epi tried them mildly but spent more time taking down directions.

When she was done, Paola said, "Make sure you do these before and after your runs."

"Thanks, sis," Epi replied.

Paola smiled and asked him to close the door as he left. She still wondered what his real reason was, but she shrugged and went back to listening to her music.

Epi decided to run with his sister's idea, literally. He began to run MORE than he usually did, which, in reality, meant to actually run since he did none anyway. He was never known for his endurance. Epi did have quick feet. In football, he made quick dashes for a first down. In kickball, Epi always made a good shot at making it "safe," from home to 1st, or 3rd to home. What he really wanted to work on was the long-distance speed that Milo, Travi, and Cinco had.

His first attempt at running practice was to get up in the morning to do some running through his neighborhood: La Loma. La Loma meant "The hill or hillside." It described the area where Epi lived as hilly, with many ups and down through the streets. Even though he had taken detailed notes about how to start a running practice from his sister, Epi decided to not follow her advice when she said that he should stretch first. He thought riding his bike away from the house and around the corner, so no one could see him run, was stretching enough. However, not knowing that you exercise differently with different activities, he would feel the error of his decision right away.

He began his running by choosing a block that he always thought looked like the track from school—four quick turns. Epi also knew it was far enough from the house so no one in the family could see him. He determined he could do two laps around this little block and that would be enough. He woke up early the next morning and rode his bike to the spot. He locked his bike to the street sign at the corner and started his first run.

He felt the tough breathing within the first half-lap, but he figured that was natural, so he pushed forward. By the next turn, ¾ into his first lap, he felt that tight feeling in the back of his legs. It was at that time he knew he should have stretched like his sister told him. A few more steps and he was hobbling. He walked the last part of his only lap and made it to his bike again. He unlocked it and slowly, very slowly walked home.

His Ma asked him where he was so early. Before he could come up with an answer, she noticed he was somewhat limping and grew concerned.

"¡Ay, mijo! Did you fall? Did you hurt yourself?! Did you get dirty?!" she questioned as she examined him. "You're not dirty. What happened?" she asked him.

"I didn't fall, Ma. I just hurt my leg...uh...riding too fast. I got up early because I..uh...I wanted to try out the new parts on my bike Pop got from The Ranch," he answered. Like with his sister, he wasn't willing to share his goal with anyone yet.

The rest of the day he stretched his sore muscles and applied Vico's Very Hot Rub to the back of his legs. Epi could feel the heat on his muscles, and it smelled like it was working. He remembers Ma putting it on his chest when he had a chest cold.

Epi rode his bike around the neighborhood for a few more days before he decided to give his training another try. When he felt he was ready, he spent a good time stretching just like Paola had taught him. He found out that those stretches weren't as easy as they appeared from his notes.

When he did the toe touches bending forward, he felt like he was meeting his ten toes for the first time. It was a slow greeting, though. The first couple of times he was only able to get close to his knees. Regardless, he felt better in the back of his legs.

Next were his leg lifts. This one he had to bend his knee and grab his ankle behind him in order to stretch the front of his legs. The first five tries he couldn't catch his foot as he kicked it backwards. When he did, he couldn't keep his balance, even falling once or twice. He figured out he could hold onto the street sign for balance, and it finally worked.

"I'm almost ready," he thought.

The calf stretches were the easiest since all he had to do was lean against the pole and bend one knee in at a time. It felt like it gave each calf a good stretch.

When he was done with the two sets each Epi thought he had already completed his workout.

It dawned on him, "Oh! I still have to run."

He made sure his bike was locked and started out.

"Here I go," he told himself.

Epi was running at a good pace. He knew if he wanted to build speed, he would have to practice. However, running at this pace, he didn't get more than two blocks before he was tired out. Adding to his problem was that he had chosen the direction in the neighborhood that was mostly uphill, so it was more like climbing a staircase than running. He was huffing and puffing going up the last hill. Epi took several huge breaths then walked back toward his bike. He unlocked his stuff and tried riding home—it was a chore. He determined that wouldn't work today so he got off and walked home again.

The next morning, he decided to go the other direction. He did his stretches and they seemed to go better than the day before. He locked up his things and started off again. He paced himself a bit better this time but wanted to continue to focus on speed. The first street on his new running path was more of a downgrade so it felt comfortable. Around the next turn however, the slope took an even steeper angle down. Epi was determined to keep going. He knew he only made it a few blocks yesterday and today he would go farther.

At first, the more downhill aspect of the street worked for Epi. That was until it went too much downhill. He felt speed on that run, but it was more due to his almost rolling down the street. As he reached his tiring point, Epi had to grab a hold of the street sign to stop. He had made it three blocks this time, but he believed he had not made any real progress. The added insult was now Epi had to walk uphill to get back to his things. This plan was not going well.

His next idea was to do his running in the evenings. He thought he would have to wait until it was cooler which meant since it was summertime, he would have to wait until it got dark. This made sense to him until he pondered further.

"Dark?!" he thought, "Uh, NO, La Llorona is out there, and I'd miss dinner."

Ma always had dinner ready at the same time - the time Pop got home from work. Besides it being a family rule to be at dinner together, missing Ma's food was not something he could do. Epi knew he had to scratch that idea.

"Am I never going to get fast enough?" Epi sighed.

As he sat on his bed after another unsatisfying morning workout and a shower, Epi had a sunken look. He heard Milo come running down the hall. Milo jumped in and out of the door to their room, as if he'd just caught a pass and dodging tacklers. In the end, he crossed the entry like he scored the winning touchdown.

He looked at his little brother, always the athlete and asked, "Milo, how is it you and I are brothers, and you are smaller and faster?"

Milo, surprised by the question, simply answered him, "I don't know. Um, I just am. Ma tells me that I was the quickest born of us three. Pop reminds me that soon after I started walking, I was running everywhere. I guess that's who I am."

Epi heaved a huge sigh. "I guess that's right. Ma always said I was the biggest baby of all of us and took the longest to be born. Pop tells me that I would always be the last one in the car to go somewhere or the last one out of Tia's house when it was time to go home."

"Yeah, Epi," Milo added, "but they also told me that because I ran as a baby kid so much I would bump into things and get hurt or break something. They also said that it was forever a problem to get me back from the jungle gym or the swings so we could go home. I would run away laughing. Pop would have to chase me down."

Epi let out a loud laugh as he remembered Pop and Paola chasing Milo around the merry-go-round at the park when they were both younger.

Milo continued "What I remember, though, is you always with your nose in some book or reading a sign we had just passed. You couldn't help but want to know what it said or what it meant. You keep getting all those good grades so it must pay off for you. I guess that's who YOU are. You can always get faster, or jump higher someday, but I agree with Pop. He tells us all the time, '*Tienes que hacer tu mismo/* you have to be yourself.'"

Epi let the words sink in and it made sense. He felt a little better and knew he wouldn't give up trying. Epi also knew that he was happy with himself.

It was another warm, sunny summer afternoon and the Ice Cream Truck was at the corner again. The gang looked around for Epi as they each reached the truck and bought their treat. They didn't see him. Milo reached them almost at the last minute on his bike, but his big brother was nowhere to be seen.

Boni asked, "Where's Epi?" as she looked past Milo toward the park.

Milo jumped off his bike and shrugged his shoulders. He rushed to the Ice Cream truck and ordered his two scoops of vanilla ice cream with gummy worms. He turned back to the gang who were all still wondering where their friend was.

Cinco asked, "Is he not coming today, Milo? You didn't buy him his sandwich this time." They all waited for his answer.

"He left the house walking at the same time I rode off. He said he'd rather walk today then he said he'd meet me here.

Before I could ask him anything, he turned a different way at the corner."

Suddenly, Travi yelled out, "There he is!" pointing down the street on the park side.

Of course, he hadn't finished his last bite of his Fudge Stick. His wild gesture as he spoke sent it flying across the table, hitting Cuatro and Boni.

They both screamed, "TRAVI!"

"Sorry," he said sheepishly. Boni put her hand out and Travi walked slowly toward her and handed back the straw wide-brimmed hat she wore that day.

As Epi came closer, all the kids ran over to meet him.

Cinco was first to greet him "Where were…" then suddenly changed his question, "What are you eating?!"

Everyone shared his curiosity. Their eyes fixed on what Epi had in his hand. He was enjoying what appeared to be a large fruit ice bar.

Epi took another taste of his frozen treat, then answered, "It's a Los Flores Paleta!" [3] He bit a piece off the top of his icy delight in front of everyone. Even Milo was surprised at Epi's ice bar.

Epi could see that the gang was still scratching their heads and eye-balling his fruit bar.

He explained, "My plan was to get faster by doing some running training so I could always catch the Ice Cream truck, right?"

Everyone nodded.

---

3   Mexican-style popsicle, usually with fresh fruit embedded

Epi continued, "I tried doing my runs in the morning, but that didn't work. I didn't want to do at night because it might get dark while I was out there. I finally told myself I would try in the afternoon. When I figured out it just wasn't working for me, I stopped one afternoon and headed for home. That day, just around the corner from here."

He pointed in a direction away from the park but close to his house.

"I ran into the Paleta man from *Los Flores Paleteria*.[4] He told me about what he was selling then I asked him why he didn't go by the park. He said that he and the Ice Cream Truck had an agreement for different areas to sell."

Everyone nodded their understanding, but a little disappointed.

"But now that we know where he is…" stated Cinco, excitedly.

"Exactly!" agreed Epi, "He's still there if you guys want one."

"Yeah!" cheered everyone.

They all gathered their bikes and wondered whether they should ride to catch the Paleta man, like they do the Ice Cream Man. Suddenly, Cinco had a thought. He asked Epi, "If you were walking, how did you catch the Paleta Man's truck?"

With that question, everyone else turned to Epi for the answer.

Walking at a normal pace down the sidewalk ahead of them, Epi answered, "He doesn't have a truck."

A collective "Huh?" came from the gang.

_____
4   Ice cream shop

Epi clarified, "The Paleta man walks and pushes a small cart full of his paletas. That's how I could catch him." He smiled and took the last bite of his fruit bar. As he walked, he thought of Hermes again. "Wasn't he the Greek god of travelers, too? That works for me." He licked the last flavor from his fingers.

5

You Are Either One or the Other

One thing that always happened for most school-age kids at the end of summer was school shopping. It was exciting: new clothes, new shoes, the latest fashions...maybe. Epi and his siblings knew that at times the new school year came up quicker than the family budget was ready for it. Because of that, they would go school shopping on the weekend after Pop's monthly payday. They didn't mind too much. Going shopping as a child, for Epi, was a hit-or-miss adventure. If his Pop took him, which was a rare occasion, he had a better chance of liking his new school clothes. However, when his Ma took them, a trip to the department store turned out a bit frustrating.

Epi and Mom were driving around the parking lot in front of the *JC & Bill's* Department Store. Ma had a tendency to "hunt" for the best parking spot, even it meant taking up to 30 minutes to find it.

On the third lap around, Epi looked up at the huge department store, and asked his Ma, "Why do we only go to *JC & Bill's* for school clothes? What about *Miller's* or *Brock's?*"

She answered, "*Ay!*" [1] with a stern look. Epi knew when Mom said "Ay!" there would be a reprimand.

She continued, "*¿Por que?* [2] *JC & Bill's* has what you need. They have your size, *Panzón.*" [3]

That was her way of reminding Epi that no other department store carried the distinctive children's size: **HUSKY**. Adult clothing could have number sizes: pants could be in 36 waist/ 30 inseam for a man or a size 4 for a woman. However, when it came to school clothes, a child had to be categorized into either Slim or Husky. Apparently, Epi, as a well-fed young man, was the latter.

While going around the lot one more time before his Ma settled on the right place to park, Epi drifted back to this morning at Paco's Tacos. He was there at the lunch tables hanging out with his friends: the twin brothers, Cuatro and Cinco.

Epi walked over to where his friends were playing the game "Don't Knock It." He sat down and watched. The object of the

---

1   An exclamation, like "Hrumph"
2   Why?
3   Chubby Kid, his nickname

game was to move a piece from the bottom of the stack of blocks to the top without making the tower fall.

Epi didn't know why Cuatro continued to play against his brother "You know he wins all the time," he said to himself.

There was something about Cinco and his ability to organize and see how things went together that made him excellent at this game.

Cuatro giggled as he watched his brother begin to move a piece from the stack. "I wouldn't do that," he said.

Cinco just gave him a side glance. He poked at the block, watched the movement of the tower, then proceeded to remove the block. The tower wobbled but Cinco took the block out and moved it to the top effortlessly.

Cuatro gasped then focused on the remaining pieces. He rushed in and moved the block of his choice. The tower fell over and toppled onto the ground. Cuatro sadly put his head down to his chest while Cinco crossed his arms in victory. Epi just shook his head.

As Cuatro picked up all pieces, Cinco scooted over on the bench toward Epi.

"Hey Epi, what're you up to?" he asked.

Epi tossed a block back to Cuatro as he answered, "Nothing much. Just killing time before I go school shopping."

"Whoa! Nice. My Mami and Papi have been so busy with the truck, we haven't gone yet either. My big sis and her husband are going to take us tomorrow. I love getting new clothes for school, don't you?" exclaimed Cinco.

"I do, too. It's just this time I have to go with my Ma. Her idea of what school clothes should look like is nuts, man. I wish I was going with my Pop. When he can take us, we end up with some 'cool' clothes," said Epi.

Puzzled, Cinco asked his friend, "What happens when your Ma takes you?"

Epi explained, "Let's just say her view of what 'fits' me isn't real and the styles are nowhere near 'cool'."

"What about your brother? What does she pick for him?" wondered Cinco.

"He gets the same treatment, but the clothes fit him a bit better. Also, somehow the shirts and colors look more like something a kid should wear. Mine look like what a circus performer would wear for their performance," explained Epi. "To top it off, this year, Milo received a bunch of clothes for his birthday. Ma told him he was good for school, and he was OK with that. So, I am on my own this time."

Shaking his head in confusion, Cinco asked, "Can't you just convince her to let you pick your own clothes?"

With a deep sigh, Epi replied, "Do you remember the story we heard in class about that guy Sisyphus?[4] He was stuck forever having to roll a huge boulder up a hill and at the very top it would magically fall out of his hands and roll back down. He'd then have to start all over again after that."

Cinco nodded.

---

4 D'Aulaire, Ingri; D'Aulaire, Edgar Parin. *D'Aulaires' Book of Greek Myths.* Delacorte Press, 1992.

"That's what it's like trying to convince my Ma I can pick out my own clothes."

As Epi and Mom entered the Boys Clothing section, his eye spotted some jeans, some new tennis shoes, and t-shirts with his favorite characters on them. He envisioned himself feeling and looking good on the first day of school when the image was broken by his Ma's shriek.

"Oy, Mijo! Look! Here are some nice pants." She would hold them up to him from behind, "Go find the shirt that goes with it."

With eyes as wide as soup bowls, Epi grunted, "Ma! Those are the color of Big Pa's old truck: rust." In truth, the pants did resemble that faint color between a faded red and wet sand.

She scowled at him, "No, they're not. They're a nice color. Go find a shirt that matches."

Walking away sullen, knowing he would probably have to wear those pants to school soon, he wondered, "I'm not sure why she orders me like it's a super science finding a shirt for these pants."

At the time *JC & Bill's* had a children's clothing line where, in order to find the proper size, you matched the animal character from the bottoms or tops to the character of its partner. They called it *Zoo Kids*. However, according to Epi, it had one "big" fault with its concept.

Epi stopped at a different rack where he found a shirt he liked. It was a solid blue short-sleeve tee with stripes down the sleeve and the bicycling team logo on the front. He knew it was not a match, but he was hopeful Ma would get it for him.

He shouted to Ma, who was stuck looking at the *Zoo Kids* rack. "I found one. I like it!" He held up the blue t-shirt.

Ma shook her head and said, "Panzón, that doesn't match. Did you check the tag?"

Epi frowned. "No. I just like it. I like the color."

Ma reprimanded him, "But Panzón, if it's not the right animal match it's not your size. You have to find the right animal for your pants. Remember it's the Happy Hippo or The Smiling Elephant. That's for the Husky kids."

And there it was. The logic to the *Zoo Kids* concept: Big animals for Big kids.

The rest of the afternoon, Epi and Ma went from rack to rack to fitting room. Epi's protests at various styles and colors Ma chose went unheard. He found himself trying on a bright yellow collared polo shirt with, believe or not, pants of the same color. The next outfit was a pale red—Epi didn't want to call it pink—and the bottoms were a painter's pant-style with all kinds of pockets. Epi wondered if these weren't leftover costumes from Halloween.

Epi thought he found himself lucky when the two worst looking sets of clothes, in his opinion, didn't fit well or didn't have his size available. Ma said they would take the tops and come back for the pants. He sighed. Two other outfits that were to Ma's liking were also placed in her shopping basket, which made Epi feel like the next week of school was going to be disastrous.

As they headed to the cashiers, what Ma did next turned Epi's sad shopping day to a triumph.

"I am saved," he thought, with a sigh of relief.

Later that day, Epi was in his yard tossing the football around with his little brother, Milo.

Travi, rode up on his bike. "Hey Epi! Hey Milo!"

The boys greeted their friend. Milo did a little extra by wiggling the football at Travi. Travi scowled back at him and pointed at his World Cup Soccer t-shirt.

Epi intervened before the silent gestures became a full-blown argument, "What's up, man?"

Travi turned to Epi, "Where've you been? I rode by here earlier today and no one was home."

Epi answered, as he threw the football back to Milo, "Milo went to the grocery store with Paola and I went school shopping with my Ma today."

"Yeah, cool. Did you get some good stuff?" Travi asked.

Milo let out a slight laugh. He threw the ball back to Epi.

As he caught the pass, Epi growled, "No. Same old stuff I get every year for school. Everything from *JC & Bill's*."

"Ok, but their stuff isn't too bad," Travi replied. He thought of the bright orange sweatshirt his abuela got him last year from there. He liked it.

Epi threw the ball again and Milo jumped up, caught it then slammed it on the ground.

"Uhhh, maybe. Some of it is not bad, I guess. A couple of shirts we brought home that were on sale were nice. For the other stuff, one good thing came out of it," said Epi.

"What?" asked Travi.

Epi replied, "She decided to put it all on layaway."

Travi scratched his head in confusion.

Epi continued, "Which means at a payment of $2 a week I won't have to wear any of it until I'm 25!"

Pondering it for a minute, Travi smiled, and came to the conclusion that Epi won his fight with the boulder.

6

La Llorona

The sun had been shining all day Saturday leading to a great afternoon of bike riding over hills, through alleys and around the neighborhood. With the day winding down, the gang all ended up at their favorite hangout: Paco's Tacos taco truck.

"What do I order today?" Epi thought to himself. He loved the food here at the taco truck and knew anything would be delicious. Still, he pondered the menu, nonetheless.

On the other hand, Travi and Milo raced to the window to see who could order their snack first. The competition between these two friends was always in high gear.

Just as the kids were finishing their plates of tacos, nachos, and drinks, they all looked up and saw the streetlights flashing. A collective panic came over them. They all knew when it got dark, they must go home and that was when the streetlights came on. The gang had memorized the signal: flicker, flicker, flicker!

With a sudden nervousness, Epi yelled at the group: "Move! We have to get home! Milo! Let's go!"

No one was startled at Epi's outburst. It was more of an awakening. The kids all jumped into action. Milo who was already ahead of everyone, yelled back at his brother, "I'm way ahead of you, dude!"

Everyone else shouted a myriad of "See ya" and "Bye" and "Later" as they rode off. Cuatro and Cinco waved to everyone as they cleaned the tables and got ready to help their dad for the evening. Paco looked out from the rear door of the taco truck, waved to the kids, and smiled at his own two boys.

After a vigorous ride around corners and up steep roads, Epi and Milo made it home, but the streetlights were already on. As they rode up the uphill driveway to the carport, they felt they made it, but barely.

However, as they closed in on where they park their bikes near the back door, the outside light was shining brightly—not a good sign. What's worse was their Ma was waiting at the back door. The boys knew if she was at the door waiting for them then she was in her strict mode. Ma looked at them with THAT look; the one that lets all children know—no matter how old—they were in for it from their mother.

"¡Ay! ¡Mijos!" [1]

Epi said to Milo softly, "We're in trouble now." Milo nodded.

---

1   Term for a mother's son, or a young boy; 'mija' for a daughter, or young girl

It was well known that when you were from a Mexican American family, like Epi and his family, when the mom began a conversation with the Spanish utterance, "Ay" she was serious. It was like she was clearing her throat and telling us not to interrupt, at the same time. Tonight, it meant she was preparing for a serious lecture.

Ma asked with a raised voice, "Where have you been? You know you are supposed to be home before the lights come on. Ya te dije,[2] La Llorona is always out there."

Epi explained, "I know, Ma. We biked as fast as we could, and we didn't see La Llorona." He paused confidently, "She couldn't catch us anyway."

Milo added, "Yeah, we ride fast," feeling even more confident.

Ma scolded them both, "Ay no, mijos," she shook her head, "La Llorona <u>will</u> catch you if she wants. *Tu Sabes.*[3] That's what she looks for: children who are out late."

Both boys just stared at her. Ma ordered the boys to come in for dinner. Paola, was helping set the table for dinner and Pop, was already sitting. The boys washed up quickly and helped bring the drinks to the table.

They all sat down and after prayers, Milo asked, "Ma, why is she out there? What is she looking for? I don't understand."

Pop and Paola looked up from eating. They looked at each other with that look that said "Uh oh! Milo asked for it."

---

2 I already told you
3 You know

Epi remembered Ma telling him why, so he knew Milo was in for a good story. He thought, "Ma tells the tale better than anyone."

"*Pon atencion*[4] Emiliano." She was serious if she used Milo's full name.

La Llorona was a mother from a nearby pueblo that took her two children to the banks of the river one day. El área era hermosa,[5] with trees for climbing and shade for sitting. The grassy picnic area was perfect for a day's outing. From the banks, you could hear the river flow peacefully, but everyone knew to be careful of its water. The mother and her children played and played in the lovely sunny day. When they had worked up an appetite, they sat and ate their lunch. The mother thought the day could not be better. After their meal, the mother began to clear the plates and the kids went to play again. She let them go, telling them to stay close. She thought that they'll be ok, so she didn't mind when they walked out of sight. When she was done cleaning, it was time to leave for home. As she packed, she called to them. Nada.[6] She called louder. No answer. Growing worried, she ran to where she thought they were. Nadie.[7] She finally went closer to the river. When she arrived, she screamed! Their toys and shoes were near the water. She screamed again; believing her children were lost to the river. The children were never seen again. For the rest of her life her heart cried and cried, that's why she is called La Llorona, the wailing woman. No one ever knew really what happened to her after that. It

---

4 Pay attention
5 The area was beautiful
6 Nothing
7 No one

has been said by la gente[8] *that she just stayed by the river until she was gone, too. But they say she never left. She is a ghost still looking for her children. People say that sometimes at night they hear a woman crying but see no one there. Children say they see her when they are out after dark alone.*

Ma's tone changed dramatically, "THAT'S WHY YOU MUST BE HOME ON TIME."

Milo and Epi were speechless. Ma gave them one last look then finally began to eat her dinner. All this time, Pop and Paola continued eating, occasionally looking up. The rest of dinner was quieter than normal.

At bedtime, Milo couldn't get Ma's story out of their heads. As tough as it was, Milo had to bring up the scary subject again.

Milo whispered, "Eh, Epi. You awake still?"

"Yeah."

Milo asked him, "Do you believe in La Llorona? I mean really believe?"

Epi paused, "I don't know. I guess I do. Travi said he's seen her before, too, so I guess I do believe."

Milo scoffed, "But, that's Travi. You think he's really seen her?"

Epi leaned down off the top bunk to see Milo. "I was reading this book about a detective and his friend 'Sherlock Holmes and Dr. Watson' [9] in the library the other day. He says that if you remove all other possibilities, when trying to solve a problem, then the one that remains must be the truth. Did you see that

8   The people
9   Doyle, Arthur Conan. *The Adventures of Sherlock Holmes.* George Newnes, 1892.

Travi didn't laugh while telling his story? He didn't jump around like he usually does when he talks? And when it was time to go home, did you see how fast he took off today?"

Milo looked up at Epi's face and nodded in agreement.

"Then I'd say he's telling the truth," Epi said.

Milo gulped then lay back down on his bed. Epi did the same.

It was quite a while before the brothers fell asleep.

The next day the gang finished an intense game of basketball at Hamilton Park.

Weary and sweaty the friends walked over to Paco's Tacos for some water and snacks. Cinco ran ahead and grabbed a basket of tortilla chips and salsa from the truck, along with some bottled water.

Travi was chugging his sports drink from his water jug, when Milo asked him, "Hey Travi, would you tell me where you saw La Llorona?"

Travi's eyes grew wide and he spit out his drink. "What?! Who told you?!" He turned quickly to Epi, "Epi!! Ugh!" and gave him a scowl.

Epi gave him an "I had to tell him" look.

Turning back to Milo, Travi reluctantly said, "OK." He took a deep breath and began, "I...I... saw her a couple of months ago. It was still light out when I was riding home after practice. I had 2 duffle bags with me, so it was hard to bike. About halfway home near the other side of the park I really noticed it had gotten dark. I looked up and saw the streetlights were on. My Nana Lupita had already told me about *La Llorona*, but I was like, 'Meh, whatever, I can make it home.'"

Everyone else was paying close attention to Travi.

He continued, "I kept on riding, but it was getting harder. The bags kept shifting and I was tired from practice. I finally got to the point where I had to get off my bike and walk it."

Cuatro gasped. Everyone's eyes got bigger, thinking about Travi walking his bike alone in the dark.

With a big breath, Travi said, "It was when I got around the last corner of the park that it happened."

Cuatro jumped in, "What happened?!"

Travi repeated himself, "That's when it happened." He paused. Everyone was on the edge of their seats. "I saw her right by The Spooky House!"

Their jaws dropped.

The kids called the older house on the far side of the park The Spooky House. The house was one of the older houses in the neighborhood. It was a wood-planked home with reminders of the old west. Its large windows had wooden shutters, thick frosted glass, and pulldown shades. It was tall with faded green paint and a wrap-around porch. The fence that surrounded the yard was wooden, worn down, and just tall enough not to see everything inside. To add to the mystery, the gang was certain they had never seen anyone go in or out of that house. But they had seen a shadow of what looked like a woman in the windows or even possibly her sitting in a chair in a dark corner of the patio. Now with Travi's tale it added to their fears.

"There she was… A lady with long, white, flowing hair in a white gown. She was standing at the corner, near the Spooky House," said Travi, *"La Viejita!"* [10]

The group let out a collective "Oh no!" then lapsed into silence.

Finally, Milo asked, "What happened next?"

The gang quickly turned back to hear Travi's answer.

Travi replied in an excited voice, "She reached out like she was coming after me!"

Cuatro grabbed Cinco's arm, who pushed him off.

"Whoa!!" Milo asked, "Really? Then what?"

Travi, nearly screaming, "WHAT DO YOU THINK?! I booked it home!"

Everyone breathed a sigh of relief. However, they were all left wondering two things: Was *La Llorona* still out there and was she in league with the lady in the Spooky House? Needless to say, they all got home on time that night, early even, and avoided the Spooky House.

Every day for the rest of the week Epi, Milo, and everyone else made it a point to finish whatever they were doing, whatever game they were playing, with enough time to get home.

Then came Sunday. After playing all afternoon after church, Epi was heading home with Milo when suddenly he cried out.

"Oh no! Oh man! Milo! Milo!"

Milo stopped suddenly, and asked, "What Epi?"

Epi answered, "I totally forgot that I needed to do something today. I need to ride to Ronny's house. He has the last part of the

---

10   The old woman

spelling bee list I wanted to study, plus a packet of strategies from his cousin who won a spelling bee at this school. I NEED IT!"

Milo noticed the sun was beginning its path toward sunset. With real concern, he asked his brother, "Why can't HE bring it to school tomorrow?"

Epi replied, "No, he can't. He's going outta town in the morning. I need to pick it up today." Epi sat on his bike, foot on the front pedal, ready to leave in the opposite direction.

Very anxious about this predicament, Milo held Epi's handlebars, "You can't. We need to get home! You won't make it before it gets dark. Remember you have to cross The Bridge, then ride through the park!"

Epi nodded in agreement, but reassured his little brother. "I have to do it. I'll make it. You go home, Milo."

Milo looked at his brother.

"I mean it," Epi stated with a strictness.

Reluctantly, Milo gave in, "OK Epi. I'll go." Milo released his brother's bike.

Epi rode the other way toward Ronny's. The Loma was rough when it wanted to be. That day it felt like it was all uphill. The Bridge felt like it was extra tall this time around.

By the time Epi made it to Ronny's, the sun was barely visible. He talked to Ronny for a bit as Ronny placed the needed items into a paper bag Sarah, Ronny's mom, gave him. He would've normally stayed there and played a little, but he knew it was getting late. He said his goodbyes and told them to have fun on their trip.

As he rode away, Epi told himself, "I can do this. Just a quick ride through the shopping center over the Bridge then downhill all the way home." He started his ride home at a confident pace. A lingering doubt began to enter his brain, but he gripped his handlebars tighter and pedaled faster.

Epi breezed through the City Heights Shopping Center. He didn't even stop at Big Fat Donut for a snack. The Bridge was the same challenge, but he made it over fast enough.

Once on the other side, Epi took a quick breather. The fact that there was still light out and the streetlights hadn't turned on, he felt like the tough part was over. As he started off again, he thought, "Yeah I'm cruisin'. Uh-huh! There's the park! Almost Home!"

Epi was so excited he started doing little jumps off the curb. As he neared the turn around the park, he scooped the front wheel over the driveway at the last house. Suddenly, he heard... BOOM! POP!

Epi shouted out loud, "What? Oh no! No, no, no, no, no!"

He knew what happened by the sound. Epi had jumped off the curb and popped his tire on a piece of broken glass.

Epi stopped on the sidewalk and examined the tire. He let out a worried sighed, "No! Now I have to walk home. *La Llorona* is out there somewhere, and I have a way to go. I still need to get past the park and The Spooky House, too."

As he began his walk home, Epi thought of *La Viejita* who lived in The Spooky House. The kids had nicknamed the lady of the Spooky House *La Viejita* since that's what she looked like to them in the dark.

Epi thought, "Travi is fast. I am sure that's how he got away from *La Llorona* that time. He could probably outrun *La Viejita*, too, but me! I can't outrun anyone!"

Epi was nicknamed, *El Panzón*, the chubby kid, and he wore it well. He was a top pick for backyard football, but he had to admit that speed and running were not his strengths.

In this moment, he could only dwell on the fact that right now he had to look out for both *La Llorona*, and the scary woman from the Spooky House.

"I have to get home. I'll just walk on the other side when I get there."

He continued walking his bike down the street and around the park. Feeling a little better with each step forward, he suddenly noticed work being done on the park side of the street, near The Spooky House. His mild enthusiasm at thinking he could get by without having to get too close was gone.

Epi stuttered, "O.o.o.o.K," took a deep breath, "I just won't look over there." He crossed the street from the park to the houses and continued walking home. His head was turning from left to right as if on a swivel, as his fists tightened around the grips on his handlebars. As he neared The Spooky House, his speed increased. He kept his gaze focused on his goal—the street corner past the house—but nevertheless, out of the corner of his eye, the shadows around the front porch loomed close. After a few more minutes of walking hastily, his breath grew heavier...

"I did it! I got passed it. *La Viejita* didn't get me! And I'm almost home and *La Llorona* didn't get me either!" His steps were quicker and lighter. As Epi turned onto the next street toward home, he stopped in his tracks. "Whoa!!"

In the early evening light, he could see a small silvery figure in a white gown. Long pale-white hair hung down over her shoulders and partly in her face. Epi was so frightened, almost frozen.

"It's HER! LA LLORONA!" He gulped. In a slight whisper, "It's true. it's true!"

Epi was stuck to the spot. The figure in front of him moved slowly closer to him and mumbled something. He could not bring himself to run, walk, or even jump away. As he squeezed the handlebars of his bike so hard the grips twisted in his hands, he could only watch her edge, closer and closer.

He prayed under his breath. "Oh, *padre nuestro*,[11] I am so sorry for not going home when I should have. Please save me. I promise I will be on time from now on." He performed the Sign of the Cross 3 times.

Epi thought, "This is it!" But as she came into the streetlight, he noticed something.

"La Llorona is wearing fuzzy pink *chanclas*?[12] And socks? Huh?" Thinking of Sherlock again, he figured this can't be La Llorona, but he was confused as to who was walking toward him. Eliminating one possibility, his look suddenly got scared again, "Wait! This is La Viejita, the lady from The Spooky House."

He was about to start praying again when he looked her over one more time. The streetlamp showed Epi that it wasn't a

---

11   Our Father
12   Slippers

ghostly gown that she was wearing but an *abuela's* nightgown. She was not floating on air. She was walking in socks and chanclas. Breathing a sigh of relief, he admitted to himself, "She's not spooky at all."

"She looks kind of like somebody's abuelita," [13] He leaned in a little and asked himself, "What is she saying?"

La Viejita whispered very softly, "Mijo, *¿dónde está mi casa?*" [14] She just stared at Epi with the look of a lost child.

Epi bent down to hear this small grandmother's soft question.

Epi repeated it back to her, "¿Donde esta tu casa? Are you lost?" She nodded and quietly answered, "Yes."

Now moved to help this elderly woman, Epi answered, "Oh, I know where you live. I will take you home, señora."

For the first time, Epi saw her smile. As he took her hand, he said to her "Oh you're cold. Here. Here's my sweater." Epi gently placed his sweater over her shoulders. "Let's get you home." She smiled again.

This new pair of friends walked back down the street for a few minutes. *La Viejita* held Epi's arm with both hands. He felt bad for thinking she was an evil spirit. He knew now she was a nice older lady. As they turned toward the park and her house, a woman excitedly came running toward the pair.

She screamed, "*¡Ama! ¿Dónde andabas?*" [15] We've been looking for you for over an hour. We came to visit for dinner, and you were gone."

---

13   Little grandmother
14   Where is my house?
15   Mother! Where have you been?

Epi, hesitant to intrude, said "She was walking down the street. I found her and walked her home. She was cold." He walked her toward her daughter's hand.

The young woman smiled, took her mother's hand, and told Epi, "Thank you so much mijo, for taking care of her. This is my mom, Doña Rita. My name is Teresa, and this is my husband, Enrique." Epi shook their hands. She paused and looked at him again, "You're Reyna and Emanuel's son, yes? We've seen you all at church. What's your name, mijo?"

Epi greeted them both, and introduced himself, "I am Epifanio; they call me Panzón, I mean they call me 'Epi,' (he blushed, Teresa and Enrique smiled) "I remember you, too. Is Doña Rita OK?"

Teresa answered, "Yes, Epi, she is, but lately she gets a little forgetful. We've been checking on her a little more regularly. She loves this house and doesn't want to leave. My sister, Norma, and I are getting her a nurse to stay with her daily. Thank you again." Teresa looked around and noticed it had turned into evening already. "It's getting dark out, mijo. If you want a ride home, I can ask Enrique to put your bike in the truck and take you home."

Epi, hesitantly admitted, "I really thought Doña Rita was *La Llorona*, but I know now she's not." With a sheepish smile, he blurted out his answer, "That means she is still out there and it's dark now, so YES I would like a ride home."

Teresa, smiled at his explanation, "La Llorona?" Teresa looked at her husband Enrique. As he loaded Epi's bike into the back of the truck, he gave his wife that "It might be true" look and winked.

Epi replied, "Yes she snatches kids away after dark. She's always out; always by the river, you know? My Ma told me about her."

Smiling even larger now, Teresa assured Epi, "Mijo, I am sure you are safe for now. Let's get you home." Enrique started the truck and Epi opened the door to the truck cab and sat down. Teresa and Doña Rita waved at them from the porch as the truck pulled away.

As Sr. Enrique and Epi drove up the driveway to Epi's house, Ma and Pop rushed out to greet them. They were both worried that Epi was so late. Milo had told them where he had gone, but no one expected him to take so long. They were a bit surprised to see Sr. Enrique drive up and Epi get out of the cab.

Ma right away asked Epi, "Ay, Panzóncito,[16] are you OK? Did you get dirty?"

Milo and Epi rolled their eyes.

Epi answered, "No, Ma. I'm fine, and I didn't get dirty."

Milo had told Ma and Pop where Epi had gone and why. Ma gave him a stern look for having thought he could make it before dark, then gave him a big hug. Pop looked down at Epi with a nod, which felt like he was saying "Not a good idea, but I understand why you went." Pop definitely had his own way of understanding Epi.

To be sure, Ma and Pop were happy to see Epi home safe, even more so after Sr. Enrique told them what had happened and why he was giving Epi a ride. They thanked Enrique for giving him a ride home.

---

16   This is Ma's cute version of El Panzón. It means "my little Panzón."

They all said their goodbyes, including Epi, and sent greetings to Doña Rita. Sr. Enrique said he would pass the greetings along and drove off.

Ma and Pop told Epi that they were very proud of their little Panzón for being so good to Doña Rita.

"Tomorrow we are having enchiladas for my little Panzóncito." Ma announced to the family.

"Thanks Ma," Epi said blushing. He smiled a big smile. Milo looked at his big brother and wondered if his smile was so big because he felt good about helping Doña Rita or for the enchiladas.

That night as they lay in their bunks Milo asked Epi, "Hey! You still awake?"

Epi grunted.

"Tell me the truth. You saw La Llorona, didn't you? You told Ma and Pop no, but I think you did."

"No, really, Milo. I was trying to get home and I saw Doña Rita. I walked her back to her house and Señor Enrique brought me home."

Feeling an odd sense of relief, Milo concluded, "Oh, so there is no La Llorona then, right?"

Epi, sprung up and leaned over the bed to Milo below him, "I didn't say that. I think she's out there. Just because Doña Rita wasn't her doesn't mean she isn't out there." He looked directly into Milo's curious eyes then rolled back to lie down.

After taking a big gulp, Milo told his brother, "Whoa! You were lucky then."

"Yeah man," said Epi, "I'll be on time from now on."

"Me Too!" vowed Milo, "Good night."

"Good night."

The next day at school was Project Day so all the gang were busy in their classrooms completing each project and presenting in front of the class. It took everything Milo had to keep his promise to Epi to not "blab" the story at school and distract them from their projects. However, Epi didn't say anything about AFTER school.

As everyone gathered at Paco's Tacos, Milo jumped off his bike, let it fall and nearly screamed, "Guys! Boni! Epi met La Llorona yesterday... and lived!!"

Everyone cried in unison, "What?!"

The entire gang stared at Epi when he rode up a few minutes behind Milo.

As he stopped his bike, Epi was a bit confused with everyone staring at him.

Travi was the first to ask, "You did it?! You really survived?! You stood up to La Llorona?"

Stuttering, Epi repeated, "I... stood up to... La Llorona?"

"See! He confirmed it! YAY!" shouted Travi.

Everyone shouted with him, "Congratulations!" There were whoops and hollers for Epi, as if he was the knight that slayed the dragon in their storybooks.

Feeling the need to clear things up, Epi interrupted their celebration, "Wait! Wait, WAIT!" Everyone quieted down suddenly. Epi turned to Milo and said slowly and intensely "What did you say?"

Milo confidently answered, "You only said not to say anything DURING SCHOOL. It's AFTER school now, so I just told them what you did."

He frowned at Milo. Epi turned to the gang and started to explain, "Hey, listen, I didn't face La Llorona."

Everyone gave him a "I don't get it" look.

He continued, "But I did meet *La Viejita.*" Everyone gave him that wide-eyed stare again.

Epi sat down at one of the picnic tables near Paco's. The gang crowded in around him. Epi began the tale of coming home late the day before and of popping his bike tire. He recounted how he met Doña Rita and that he truly thought she was *La Llorona*. He told them of how he thought at that moment he was a goner. The kids hung on every word, even Milo, who had heard the story multiple times.

Epi explained he realized Doña Rita was lost, he helped her home and met her family. He shared how in the end he thought she looked like their own *abuelitas* and how she was a nice older lady who just needed to be taken care of.

With a sense of relief, everyone smiled at Epi and began chattering among themselves.

"Oh and, for the record, I do think *La Llorona* is still out there," Epi stated. "Just have to say that."

Everyone gasped and all agreed with his declaration.

From then on, every time the gang rode by Doña Rita's house, they'd wave at her or ring their bike bells. Many times, she'd be outside with her nurse or family. Sometimes she'd be at the window but every time she'd look up and smile.

For years, the gang would do everything they could to be home on time. Sometimes early, sometimes barely making it but no one ever stayed out alone late enough to worry about *La Llorona*.

In truth, it would be a long time before any of them realized there was no river near La Loma for *La Llorona* to wander.

Still, it got them home on time anyway.

7

Top Dog

I t was about 5:00 in the morning on Saturday. Epi was sleeping soundly until Pop came in.

"Get up mijo. You're coming to work with me today."

Somehow Epi knew this was coming. As his head swam between asleep and awake, he tried to find some way to get out of this. Nothing came to mind, but he knew exactly how this idea got started. Let's go back to Monday.

Boni, not usually one to trail behind any of the gang when riding her bike, was struggling to keep up with Epi today.

"Slow down Epi!" yelled Boni as he madly pedaled home, "What's the deal?"

Epi showed no sign of slowing down, "I can't! I'll call you later." He rode on ahead of everyone.

Epi rode up the driveway, threw his bike down, and ran through the back door. "Ma! Ma!"

"Quiet Epi! I'm on the phone," said Paola, Epi's big sister. She was always on the phone.

He ignored her reprimand. "Whatever. Where's Ma?"

"She's in her room. Why?"

Epi ignored the questions and ran to his parents' room. "Ma! I did it!"

She quickly put down the towel she was folding onto the neat piles on her bed, asked, "What mijo?! What did you do? Did you get hurt? Did you get dirty?"

"No, Ma. I got it! I got the Top Dog Award!"

"Really? Good for you?" Ma paused for a moment and with a confused look on her face asked, "What is that, Panzón?"

Epi explained. "I won the Top Dog Award because I had perfect attendance, the best spelling quiz score, and best grades for the month." His smile could not have been bigger. He knew by winning this award he was on his way to qualifying for the school spelling bee.

With great pride, Ma said. "Ay, mi Panzóncito, that's great news!" She grabbed him and gave him a huge momma bear hug. Epi usually pulled away from these hugs but today he paused just enough to feel the love Ma put into it.

After finally pulling away, Epi excitedly said, "Thanks Ma. I was working hard this month. There are some strong kids in my class, like Boni and Cinco. It's always tough to get all three for the month. I want you and Pop to come to the Awards

Ceremony. It's Wednesday at 11:00 in the morning!" He couldn't contain his excitement.

The look on Ma's face was a mixture of glowing pride and slight sadness. "Wednesday, Epifanio?" she asked. "OK, mijo." She paused for a deep breath then continued, "You know *tu papá* [1] is always so proud of what you kids do, but he works all day, every day. He doesn't miss work because he can't."

Not fazed one bit, Epi replied, "I know Ma, but this is a big deal. Pop knows how much I've been studying for the big spelling bee and this is one more step toward that. I know he'll come." He took another deep satisfying breath thinking about his parents both attending the ceremony. "I'm going to tell the gang. I'll be back for dinner. Don't tell Pop, please. I want to tell him." Epi rushed out still filled with all the excitement of this award-winning day.

"But Panzón..." Too late he was gone.

Ma's face was filled with more worry than before. She knew Epi was excited about this award, but she wondered what would happen if Pop didn't make it.

Epi rode his bike over to the park to see the gang. His head was swimming thinking about the coming award ceremony.

Seeing his brother ride up then park his bike at the racks, Milo announced, "Here he comes. Ha ha! He looks like he's walking on air."

Turning around at Milo's proclamation, Travi began to laugh, as well, "You should've seen him in class when Ms. Nikols

---

1   Your dad

told him." Travi jumped up to imitate Epi, chest puffed out, "Who?! Me?!"

With loud giggling and laughter, the kids walked around with their chests out, acting as if they had just won the award.

Epi reached the tables. "Hey!" he said smiling from ear to ear.

As they all turned to greet Epi, Cinco started first, "Drum roll, please!" Everyone started slapping their hands and legs on the table.

Cinco continued "...for his Excellency *El Perro Grande*[2]...*Señor Epifaniiooooooo!*"

They all bowed, clapped, and cheered.

Epi was slightly embarrassed. "Whatever, you guys."

Cinco shook his head, "No, man. That's a Big Deal!"

Cuatro, came from the other side of the truck, "EPI! I heard you won! That is awesome!! I mean really!" He hugged Epi.

Epi, as he escaped Cuatro's emotional squeeze, replied, "Thanks, Cuatro. I was surprised but it felt good!"

"Great job, Epi," said Boni.

"Thanks, Boni. I know if you hadn't gotten sick, you…"

Boni interrupted, "No you earned it. How'd your mom take it? I bet she was excited."

Epi's eyes gleamed, "Yes, she was. She's going to be there on Wednesday with my Pop."

Upon hearing Epi explain that their Pop was going to the ceremony, Milo asked Epi, "She said that? I've never seen Pop miss work. Are you sure?"

_____

2   Big Dog

Epi, full of confidence, replied, "Yeah, I'm sure. I told her how important it was, and she agreed with me."

Still wondering, Milo questioned, "OK, Epi, but I'm just saying."

"I hear you but you're wrong," Epi countered.

Changing the subject, Cinco invited them all to the truck. "Forget it for now. My dad said everyone gets 2 tacos for free for Epi's award."

When Paco offered food, no one wasted time getting there. Everyone ran to the truck.

It was Tuesday night at dinner. Eating dinner together was always a rule in Epi's house. Occasionally, Pop would barely make it, but no one would eat until everyone was sitting down.

Pop arrived right on time. Epi and Milo met him and did their coming home ritual. Epi was beaming with a desire to remind his Pop about his award ceremony the next day, but Ma signaled to wait until they had dinner. Reluctantly, Epi did as he was told.

Ma, as she always did, made sure everyone was served before she sat down. When she did, everyone bowed their heads for the blessing.

"Amen!"

Everyone dug into the steaming frijoles and arroz, then each picked their tacos off the plate. Pop, at the head of the table, filled his tacos with more cheese, and some of Ma's famous but super *chiloso*[3] salsa.

3　Spicy

After a few bites, Pop asked about everyone's day. Epi, jumping at the chance, was cut off by his sister sharing what her new work schedule would be at the movie theater and that she was saving her money for the Prom. Pop smiled at Paola's description of her dress and shoes.

Next, Epi was about to open his mouth, when Milo jumped in and told Pop about the three touchdowns he had scored at school during recess.

Pop laughed and asked, "Only three today, Emiliano?"

Milo quickly retorted, "We got out to recess late today so I didn't have enough time for more!"

Pop smiled at him. He knew Milo took his football playing seriously, even at his age, and he loved to tease him about it.

"¿Y tu Epifanio? How was your day?"

Epi looked at Ma, who seemed to reluctantly give Epi the OK to say something.

Hardly able to contain his excitement, Epi blurted out, "So Pop, remember, it's at 11:00 a.m. in the cafeteria yeah? You and Ma will have seats saved for you. They will do the younger grades first so you may have to wait for a minute before it's my turn, but it will be awesome."

Epi further explained what the ceremony would be like and the punch and cookie reception they would have afterwards., Everyone at the table, all had a look of concern on their faces. They all seemed to be thinking the same thing, "Poor Epi. He doesn't seem to understand that Pop WANTS to go but he just can't."

Finally, Epi finished his detailed description.

With a slight pause, Pop acknowledged, "I am very sure that the ceremony will be a great event. You and all those kids deserve these awards, mijo, I am so proud of you. But ... you know, I just can't miss work. It's the Season and the *Mayordomo*[4] needs me. He probably wouldn't give me the day off even if I asked."

Epi, still determined, tried to explain to Pop, "But Pop this is the biggest award I've ever won!" He started tearing up as he finished.

Pop tried to console Epi, "I know mijo, I know. I am sorry. We will have a big dinner for you when I get home. Ma will make your favorite. *Sí, amá?*" [5]

Ma nodded with a smile and a slight tear in her eye. She knew Epi couldn't accept it and she felt for him."

Epi started crying then sniffled, "Ok, Pop, I understand."

Epi said he understood but really, he didn't. Pop never missed work before, that's true. He worked hard every day. He never complained. He woke up every day: Monday through Saturday and worked from dawn to dusk. Everyone in the family knew that but today Epi didn't want to accept it.

On Friday as Epi and Milo were walking home, Boni caught up to them. She noticed Epi walking very slowly, slower than normal.

Boni felt the need to cheer up her friend, "Hey Epi! I have to say your Ma rocked that dinner for your award on Wednesday. Her enchiladas were awesome, as usual!"

---

4   Supervisor
5   Yes, mother?

Epi, not looking up, quietly replied, "'I know. They always are. Thanks." Any other time anyone mentioned his Ma's enchiladas, Epi would have begun to salivate like that little dog hearing the bell. This time he had no reaction.

Boni was worried. She knew Epi was still disappointed after Pop didn't show for the awards ceremony.

Knowing his brother better than most, Milo tried to get his mind off his troubles.

"Of course, we had enchiladas, Boni, their Panzón's favorite. That's why she made them. All her food is great but if Panzón wants something special, then enchiladas it is, right, Panzón?"

Milo quickly ducked because he expected a swing, or a toss of a book, or at least a loud grunt of disagreement from Epi for this teasing. Nothing. Now, even Milo was worried. He knew Epi usually reacted very quickly to his teasing; even more so when he called him "Panzón." Epi only let Ma and Pop call him that. Yet, this time Epi just ignored him.

At that moment, Travi caught up to the rest, "Did you say enchiladas? MMMMMMMM… I just finished the leftovers I took home from Wednesday. And they were YU-UH-MY." He rubbed his stomach vigorously. Travi saw Epi's expression. He could plainly recognize his friend was down-in-the-dumps, so he asked, "What's the matter dude?"

"Nothing," Epi answered, barely able to be heard.

Milo interjected, "Hey Epi. You still sad about Pop missing the awards ceremony? Come on. You knew it. He works all the time. Don't take it so hard."

"I know."

Epi knew everything everyone said was true. He just couldn't accept it. "How could Pop not want to go to his ceremony?" he thought to himself.

No matter what the gang said or did on their walk home, Epi could not be cheered up. Everyone else stopped at Paco's Tacos but Epi walked home alone. Everyone knew that Epi must have been really sad to not go to the taco truck.

Fast forward to Saturday morning

Walking by their room, Pop urged Epi, "Come on mijo. Get up, get dressed. Your mom has some breakfast and we got to go."

Barely awake, he said, "I'm up. I'm up." Epi rubbed the *lagañas* / "the sleepies" out of his eyes and rolled off the side of his top bunk. THUD. Epi hit the floor; gravity had never been Epi's friend.

Milo woke up and opened one eye, "Dude! What are you doing?"

"Pop said I am going to work with him today."

"But it's Saturday?!" Milo didn't understand and wasn't awake enough to inquire further, so he fell back to sleep.

Epi was left in the dark searching for both his shoes and the reason he had to work with Pop today. "Did I do something wrong? I won the award, didn't I? Was that not right?" Questions swam through Epi's head as he dressed and washed up.

After a quick breakfast, they got into the truck and headed off on the hour drive to The Ranch, as Pop called it. Epi fell asleep on the bench seat as Pop listened to the oldies songs he loved. Pop was the King of Oldies music. This was the music he grew up on. It was played at the dances he and Ma, and his siblings attended as teens. Despite getting up so early and going to work without knowing why, hearing Pop's music play helped Epi sleep.

The huge company farm Pop worked for was known for growing all kinds of agricultural products like cotton, wheat, and alfalfa. Pop had worked in agriculture his entire life. He now worked as a Field Machine Service mechanic. Pop said he remembered the days when he and his family worked in the fields picking cotton by hand. Now, it was harvested by huge machines driven by many of Pop and Ma's friends. His job was to supervise them and make sure the machines were running well. That's what Ma told the kids about Pop's job. What he did specifically from morning to night, Epi was about to learn firsthand.

After hearing Pop call his name, as if in a dream, Epi woke up and looked around. He was a bit confused. As he moved Pop's jacket fell off him—he must've put it on him as a blanket. Epi scooted toward the door. He quickly noticed that the interior of the truck was different. He sat up and looked around through the truck window, Epi wondered, "Where are we?"

By this time, the sun was bright, and the morning dew had dried off. Epi saw rows of plants all around, as well as other vehicles parked up the road between the fields. He could smell the cotton and other plants as well as the motor fumes from the engines nearby.

Pop walked over to the truck window and laughed. "Good morning, Epi. In case you're wondering, this is my service truck. This is what I use to do my work for the day."

"When did we change trucks?" Epi knew Pop wouldn't carry him from truck to truck—Pop would say, "Mijo, you're big," so he was confused as to when he woke up enough to get into it.

Pop smiled and explained "We got here around 6 and I woke you up a little. I thought you were awake, at least. We grabbed my work sheet for the day then we got into this truck. You don't remember?"

Epi, rubbed his eyes, "No. Sorry."

Pop, smiled again, "That's OK. Come out now. It's break time."

Epi opened the door and stepped down, and asked "What time is it?"

"8 in the morning," answered Pop.

A shocked Epi thought, "What?! 8:00 in the morning?! I slept all that time?"

Pop nodded at Epi then led him over to the group of men that sat on the tailgate of a truck. Pop had his lunch box open already with the delicious food Ma had packed for them. Epi barely remembered seeing Ma this morning in the kitchen. Still, he knew Ma got up with Pop every morning. If Pop never missed a day of work then Ma never missed a chance to send Pop off with a good breakfast, a full lunch box, and a hot thermos of coffee.

"Reach into the lunchbox and get your *taco de huevos y chorizo*.[6] Ma made some boiled eggs, too," Pop said to Epi as he poured himself some coffee. "There's some orange juice in the ice chest for you."

---

6   Small burrito of spicy Mexican sausage and egg

Epi gathered his items and found a spot next to Pop in the bed of the truck. As he sat down on a folded tarp to eat, he asked Pop, "What have you been doing since we got here? I mean, your shirt is dirty already, and your boots look like they've been in and out of the mud."

Epi could only remember what Pop looked like after work: he was usually dirty from work, head-to-toe. Pop never said from where he had gotten so dirty, he just said he had had a busy day at work. On the other hand, Epi knew Pop never left for work like that. Pop always kept himself clean and ready for any occasion. Epi was surprised to see him so dirty already in the morning.

Pop smiled and said "Working, mijo." Pop gave Epi a rundown of the past two hours: "First, I checked in with the crew in the machine shop to see if two engines were done with repairs. I then left with you in the truck and drove to the southwest section to check on the crew who was starting the picking. Afterwards, I moved three irrigation pumps. After break, I still need to go change the oil in two other pumps."

Pop took another bite of his *taco* and a sip of his coffee. He seemed to cut off his work list which made Epi think there was still more Pop would have to do for the day.

Epi knew his dad worked hard. Everyone in the family was proud of it, but Pop still came home and did work around the house. If the car needed fixing, he would work on it until it was done. If Ma said the sink was stopped up, Pop would work on that. Epi knew Pop did all the repairs around the house because he and Milo were his designated helpers. Milo would hold the flashlight and get the tools while Epi "held this or tightened that" for Pop as needed.

He thought to himself, "Pop would help even if we needed help with our homework, especially math—Pop was good at math. He'd stay with us until it was done."

It hit Epi that Pop already had a long day *before* he got home, and he *still* had enough energy to do all this. A new sense of pride came over Epi.

The rest of the day was long but more active and more exciting than he expected. Pop taught Epi how to move huge mechanical irrigation pumps. The first thing was to lift the two massive water pipes using the hydraulic machinery: one from out of the water and the other from out of the field. Pop showed Epi how to turn them. Next, he taught Epi to secure them with a huge chain that Epi could barely lift. Pop offered to do it for him. At this point Epi was determined to work hard, so he told Pop he could do it. Pop smiled at him.

Once everything was ready, Pop sent Epi up to the driving platform. He thought it was a crazy feeling to stand on the platform, hold the steering wheel, and pull the lever that moved the pump. He didn't drive it very far—one field width over—but it felt like miles long.

When it was lunchtime, they ate the rest of the lunch Ma packed for them. When they were done, it was time to work on some field engines. Pop explained they were water pumps too, but they didn't move.

He said, "We just had to change their oil today and check the fluids."

Epi didn't know what all that meant, but if it was like home working on the cars, then he knew he could help. Epi started the machinery on the truck every time Pop needed it.

When it was time to go home, Epi was exhausted. He really learned what it was to work hard. However, to Epi, the best thing was that he could now understand what his Pop did every day and how important and busy his dad was to the team and The Ranch.

As they drove home that evening, Pop looked over at Epi, and asked him, "You want a snack, Panzón? I usually stop at the store with my compadres Julio and Ramon."

Epi, still feeling tired, smiled and nodded.

They arrived at the Center St. Market on the corner of the highway that took them home from Pop's work. It was a small white building with one old fashioned gas pump and what looked like someone's home attached to the rear. Pop drove to the side to park the truck. Epi could see the trucks of Pop's friends, Julio and Ramon. These two men both worked at The Ranch, too, but at the other end.

Pop stepped out and Julio greeted Pop right away, "¡Compa! ¿Como te fue hoy? [7] Tough day?"

Pop shook Julio's hand, "No tanto.[8] Just the same but I had help today."

Epi stepped out of the truck and Pop told Epi to say hello to *Don*[9] Julio and *Don* Ramon, while he went inside to get a soda and some chips.

---

7   Friend/Buddy, how'd it go today?
8   Not too much
9   "Don" is a term of respect, like "Mr."

Epi walked over and said hello while shaking their hands firmly. Epi was taught by both Pop and Ma to be respectful to your elders and greet everyone with a firm handshake, a smile, and a hug for relatives.

Julio immediately responded to Epi's strong handshake by asking, "Oy, Mijo. You're Epifanio, yea?"

Epi nodded.

Julio continued, "You're the one your Dad told us about. ¿No, Ramon?"

Ramon nodded vigorously, and asked Epi, "You won that award, right? Good job!"

Epi smiled and quietly said thank you to them both but was very surprised.

Julio added, "Your dad talked about it all week. He told us it was because you didn't miss school, you got the best grades in the class, and you were the best speller! That's amazing. I can't spell to save my life. Right, Ramon?" He laughed.

Ramon, nearly spitting out his soda for laughing, replied, "He's telling the truth, mijo." Ramon cleared his throat and continued, "He can't spell, but you winning that award, congratulations. Your Dad was very proud."

Now Epi was completely shocked. He thought Pop didn't come because he didn't think his award was important enough to miss work. After everything they did today, it finally hit him that Pop really wanted to go but he couldn't.

Pop walked back out with the food and Epi couldn't help but smile the biggest smile at him. Pop smiled back. Epi didn't know if Pop had heard their conversation, but their little rest stop was very refreshing.

After they left the store and were driving home, Epi turned and asked "Pop, how long have you been working?"

"Today?"

"No. I mean in your life; how long have you been working?"

Pop thought for a minute then answered, "Oh! Well, since I was your age, mijo. I was working in the fields picking, pulling weeds, whatever they needed. Your tios[10] and tias[11] and I would work in the mornings and after school, even weekends as soon as we all could hold an *azadon*.[12] Being one of the oldest, I had to go to work full time when your *abuelo*[13] got hurt and couldn't work anymore. I was about your sister, Paola's age, when I stopped school and had to help the family. My first job helped pay the rent and feed the family. A couple of your tios had to, as well. That's just what we had to do to help your *abuela*[14] take care of grandpa and my other brothers and sisters."

Epi looked up and gasped, "Wow! I didn't know that. That sounds hard. Didn't you miss school? Your friends?" Epi knew that Pop came from a big family. He had 12 brothers and sisters. Ten were younger than him so being one of the oldest Pop had felt the responsibility.

"It was hard, and I did miss school. As for my friends, most of them did the same thing with me. All our families were the same:

---

10   Uncles
11   Aunts
12   Garden tool, garden hoe
13   Grandfather
14   Grandmother

big, hard-working, needing each other. But mijo, working hard for them and now working hard for you guys is what I do. You may be there someday but me and your mom just want to give you the chance to figure it out for yourselves. To be able to finish school and college, even, so that when you do work hard it'll be because you want to, doing what you want to."

Epi couldn't think of what to say. All that came out was "Thanks Pop."

Epi had visited the small town where his Pop and his brothers and sisters had grown up. Crops and small houses everywhere, along with Epi's large extended family. He loved visiting because there were all his cousins, his tios and tias, and a lot of good food. Now, that he heard this story from his Pop, he began to notice that the area was like the small farm labor camps in the Book of the Month in the School Library, The Circuit, where the author shared his life story doing work just like his Pop. His Pop was always his hero but now, Epi thought, he was like right out of one of his favorite stories. Epi felt a strong sense of pride come over him for his Pop.

The rest of the ride home Epi just paid attention to Pop talk about the music that he listened to. He did a little whistling to the tunes like Pop did but mostly Epi just let it all sink in. He thought about why Pop got up every day to do what he did. It was probably the best day that Epi ever had with his dad; mostly because he understood him that much more.

On Monday morning as the bell rang to start school at 8:00 a.m. Boni saw Epi and asked, "Hey Epi! You look better. What did you do this weekend? I didn't see you."

Epi, in a very deep voice, with shoulders back, very proud, "Me and my Pop had to work Saturday. Tough stuff but you gotta do what you gotta do."

Boni smiled back at him but with a puzzled look. Epi sat down at his desk and took out his things. He stopped for a moment and looked out the window and smiled. He took a deep breath and started the warm-up activity Ms. Nikols had written on the board.

At the same time at The Ranch, Pop was on his break. He called to his friend, "Hey Julio! ¿Como le va?" After Julio greeted him and they talked for a bit, Pop sat down to eat.

He opened his lunch box and was surprised at what he saw there. It was a rolled-up piece of paper, like a diploma or parchment. He untied the ribbon around it and saw that it was Epi's award.

When it was fully open, Pop noticed a handwritten note over the name. The note was decorated like an award. It read:

> *To Sr. Emmanuel, my Pop.*
> *Thank you for being the TOP DOG Dad.*
> *Love Epifanio, Your Panzón*

Pop set the award down on his lap. He looked up into the bright morning sun and smiled. He read the note again. Still with a huge smile on his face and just a little bit of a tear in his eye, he whispered to himself, "No, mijito, Thank you."

8

Working Hard

Today at Paco's Tacos the twins, Cuatro and Cinco were hard at work. They both loved helping their dad, Paco. They knew mom was busy studying and it was their job to help him keep the business going. The brothers may have been twins but they could not have been more different. Cuatro with all his energy was outside wearing the Taco Suit advertising to passersby. Cinco was inside the truck helping make sure all the supplies were in order and organized.

Paco was very proud of his two helper sons. Their aid in the kitchen and at the counter helped the family enormously. He appreciated their help even more recently since Annie was in some tough classes this term.

Cinco shouted to the gang from behind the Order window, "Hey you guys! Where's Epi?"

Travi didn't answer right away. He was too busy fixing Boni's hat on his head—a light blue cap with a front brim and a short material down the back to cover the neck. Satisfied with the fit, Travi answered Cinco, "I don't know where Epi is. He wasn't at his house when I came this way."

Boni tied her bandana over her head, "He said he had to go to Javier's for something." Looking at Travi, she gave him an OK sign of approval at her hat on his head.

Milo nodded his head in agreement with Boni, "He said he'd come over here when he was done."

Boni added, "It's a bummer Javier's family is moving but he said his dad got a way better job. Too bad its out of town." Everyone agreed with Boni.

Cuatro, looking out from the corner, said, "Hey! I see him... I think."

Cinco snapped at him, "What do you mean 'I think'?" He handed the customer from the offices down the street their taco plate combo, "It's either him or not."

Cuatro responded, "I know. It looks like him but...no, it's some old man in a tie." He paused then very excitedly said, "but he's walking Epi's bike!!"

Cuatro dropped the *Paco's Tacos* sign and ran at the stranger, still wearing the Taco suit. As he neared the stranger, he yelled, "What are you doing with my friend's bike?!"

When the stranger came into focus, Cuatro realized his mistake. "Oh. Epi?" totally bewildered, "Is that you?"

Epi had told his mom about possibly getting a job as a paperboy. She demanded he dress up for the interview with a tie. Of course, the only dress shirt Epi owned was his first communion shirt from a few years ago, which did not fit very well anymore. Epi was called *El Panzón* by his parents and family because he was, as his Ma put it, well-fed. In the end, he wore his dad's dress shirt which fit Epi's barrel chest but was far too long everywhere else.

Cuatro asked his friend, "Why are you dressed like that?"

Epi shaking his head, "My ma said I had to dress up to go to my appointment." He walked over to the group. Cuatro danced along behind.

Travi jabbed at Epi, "*¡Orale*,[1] Epi! Did you have to go to a wedding or a funeral or something?" He laughed. Epi growled at him.

Boni scowled at Travi. "Don't listen to him. You look nice, Epi. How did it go?" The rest of the gang waited for his answer.

Epi, hardly able to contain himself, shouted "I got it! I got the job! I am a paperboy! "

Everyone shouted," Yay!"

"Yeah, I start tomorrow; early in the morning which is cool because Pop gets up that early anyway. He can help me. I work every morning but not too long; just long enough to deliver the paper over there behind Travi's house."

Boni asked, "That's good but every day? That's a lot of work. And will you have to work on my birthday next Saturday?"

Epi replied, "Yes but it's early morning. I'll be there at your party. Count me in!"

---

1   An Exclamation like "Wow"

Boni always had the best birthday parties, from last year's petting zoo to the hypnotist two years ago who made Travi act like a chicken. It was the best of times. This year her mom, Dolores, got their favorite band *Menturu*[2] to play. Mando, the lead singer and band leader, was Dolores' brother and Boni's uncle. *Menturu* was a band made up of men from the neighborhood. They played everything the gang liked: salsa, ska, and old school.

Epi *had* to go to this year's party. He also knew it's only right to take something, a gift to a birthday party, if you could. This year he would be able to buy his own gift and one for Milo so he could go, too—he loved *Menturu* just as much as Epi. Boni never demanded a gift, but she was his friend, and she deserved a present.

Not too long ago, Ms. Nikols, Epi's teacher, had given him a book G'Morning, G'Night: little pep talks for me & you as a reward for spending time reading to younger students in the library. It was filled with short sayings that were positive messages. He was thinking of one as he explained his new job: "Good morning, you will have to say no to things to say yes to your work. It will be worth it." He thought getting up every morning—saying no to sleeping in—will be hard but if he could earn the money to be able to buy his friend a birthday gift, it would all be worth it.

Monday morning, before dawn, it was time for Epi to start his new job.

---

2   Pronounced Men-too-roo; blended word referring to reggae beats and rhythms

Pop shook Epi, "Mijo, wake up." He shook him again, "Your papers are here. Mijo!"

Epi, stirred, "I'm up, Pop. I'm up." He turned to Milo. "Hey Milo! Get up! You said you'd help me so get up."

Yawning a big yawn, Milo asked, as he rolled over, "Huh? Now?"

Epi answered, plainly, "Yes, if you wanna go to the party, this is what we gotta do."

Milo groaned but got up.

After a quick restroom break for "necessities" and cleaning, the two boys headed to the living room where Pop had a stack of newspapers on the carpet. Epi and Milo plopped down on the floor.

Epi explained to his brother, "OK, look. This is how Javier and the newspaper manager showed me how to wrap the papers with the rubber band." He demonstrated, "Fold, rubber band two times around, then into the bag; one side then the other."

Milo shot back, "That's not that bad. Watch." SNAP! went the rubber band on Milo's fingers "OW!" The rubber band had broken and slapped Milo's hand sharply.

Epi to Milo, "Don't do it that fast! You'll break the rubber bands. We have to pay for them."

"What?!" exclaimed Milo as he rubbed his hand. "We've got bills already?"

Pop explained, "Yes, mijo. You take care of your own supplies, pay the paper for your customers' subscriptions then the rest is yours." Milo raised an eyebrow but since Epi was nodding, he accepted this fact as part of the job.

Epi said confidently, "Now, we have to hurry. Everyone expects their newspaper before they leave for work."

The boys got back to wrapping the papers. Milo only snapped his fingers three more times before he got the hang of it. The boys got through all the papers and loaded the two sides of the white, canvas paper carrier bag.

Epi announced to Milo, "OK, ready to go. Help me carry it to my bike."

Milo, feeling confused, asked, "Don't you put it over your head? That's how I have seen it done on TV."

Epi demonstrated, "No, watch me. Javier said you wrap it on your handlebars like this." He showed his brother how to loosen the straps on each side of the carrier bag and wrap them tightly around the handlebars. First the right side, then the left.

Milo scratched his head, and said, "That looks tough to ride. I still say over the head."

Epi struggled a bit to get on his bike, but finally he was set. He took off down the driveway with good momentum. He rode toward the first houses, having memorized which houses to throw to and where they wanted their paper. He rode in and out of those first streets, but Epi hadn't listened close enough to Javier when he explained the best path to take. You see Epi lived on the side of town called *La Loma* or the hills and Epi had left the houses on his route that were all at the top for the end.

Working on the second half of his route, Epi found himself huffing and puffing and riding more slowly than anticipated. As he reached one of the tallest hills in *La Loma*, he was standing up pedaling, and said to himself, "How did Javier do this every day?"

At the top of the hill Epi fell on the nearest lawn. He laid there, breathing heavily, saddened. He was thinking he was not cut out for this job. Suddenly Epi heard what sounded like his bike and bag being moved. He looked up and he saw his brother.

"MILO! What're you doing here?"

Milo said, matter-of-factly, "I've kind of been following you. It's your first day and well... we're partners, ¿que no?" [3]

Epi smiled at his little brother, "Yes, we are."

He got up off the grass and Milo helped him mount the bike. Milo had brought an empty backpack and Epi filled it with rolled newspapers. Milo put it on backwards; letting it hang in front of him so he could reach into the large pocket to grab a paper and throw it. Epi took one side of each street and Milo took the other. It was a tough first day, but the two boys finished with enough time to go home, eat, and get ready for school.

Epi and Milo woke up every morning after that to deliver the newspapers. With Milo's help, Epi was able to finish each day's delivery leading up to the party. The two brothers wrapped papers together, collected dues, and delivered on time. Every once in a while, they would see someone come out to get the paper, as they rode by. The people always had a smile on their faces, waving at the paperboys.

As Boni's party drew near, Epi and Milo went with Paola to the mall. They went shopping together for two gifts for Boni. Each chose what they thought their friend would like and were very proud to pay for them with their own money.

---

3   Or not?

Finally, the day of the party arrived. Ma yelled at the boys, "*Hijos, Ya Pues!*[4] It's time to go."

Epi answered "I know, Ma. I'm waiting for Milo. Milo! Let's go!"

"I am ready!" Milo shouted as he exited the bathroom.

Ma warned, "Ay, now, behave, be nice and say Hello to her mom for us."

Epi answered, "Yes, Ma," as they ran off.

The boys raced down the block and around the corner to Boni's house. When they got there, food was being served. The first person they saw was Boni's mom, Dolores.

Dolores greeted the boys with a large smile, "Epi, Milo. I was wondering where you were."

Epi greeted her and apologized, "Sorry, we had to deliver the newspaper today then had to collect from a few customers."

Milo added, "Yeah, Ms. Dolores, we were working." He smiled proudly.

"Of course! your mamá[5] told me. So grown up." Dolores gave the boys a very motherly-proud smile, "And you both brought her gifts?!" The boys puffed their chest proudly. "Ok, put the gifts over there and grab a plate. Bonita has spots for you to sit."

Both boys thanked her and moved toward the food table. "Oh, my mom said 'Hi'," Epi told her as he walked away.

Boni, with a screech, called out "Epi! Milo! Yay! I thought maybe you weren't... I'm glad you're here."

---

4   Boys, Now!
5   Mom

Cuatro added "Yeah Epi! Glad you're here. It's time for the piñata. It's shaped like a big horse!" He grabbed the plastic bat and blindfold.

Cinco stopped him and reminded, "No, Cuatro. Remember... it got stuck in the tree." Cuatro looked puzzled.

Cinco continued, "Yeah, remember, it was stuck then Travi decided to climb up to get it...and fell."

"What?!" asked Milo, as they looked at Travi.

Travi shrugged. "I THOUGHT it was a good idea."

"He's OK," explained Cinco, "he landed on the piñata." Everyone laughed. "So, everyone got candy this time since he broke it when he fell. If you want some candy, we saved a leg from the piñata filled with candy for you both."

Epi and Milo gave out another good laugh, along with Travi and the rest of the gang!

The rest of the afternoon was all fun and games. Then came the cake. It was amazing. The cake was from the lady down the street. It was three-tiered, white frosting with pale blue and yellow trim, Boni's favorite colors. The bottom was chocolate, the second was white, and the small top tier was Boni's favorite, carrot cake. Everyone had a piece; Epi had two!

When it started getting dark, the best part of the evening was about to begin: *Menturu* was ready to play! Everyone screamed with excitement!

Mando, the lead singer of *Menturu*, stepped up to the mic. He announced to the crowd, "Thank you all for coming. We're *Menturu* and we're happy to be here to celebrate my niece's special day with all of you. This first song is for the birthday girl—Miss Bonita Esperanza! Happy Birthday mija!"

Boni turned red hearing her full name. Her *Tio*[6] winked at her as he began playing his trombone. She grew even more red, but the music made it better.

Dancing went on for hours. Travi did his "Jumping Everywhere" dance. Cuatro followed along with him. Cinco spun Boni round and round during a salsa song, while Epi and Milo showed off the steps their sister taught them. Everyone stayed dancing on the back-lawn-turned-dance floor until nearly the end.

As the festivities began to close, Mando got on the mic one last time. He announced, "And for our last song I wanna give a shout out to Epi and Milo."

The boys were stunned at hearing their names.

He continued, "These two boys get up early every morning and deliver the newspaper to all us neighbors. I especially want to thank them for getting my *abuelo*[7] his paper every morning in time for his coffee. It means a lot to him. It means a lot to me. Thanks, *mijos*." [8]

Epi and Milo beamed. They didn't think their little job was much. They delivered the newspaper. The boys had discovered it really did mean something to their neighborhood. Mando's "Thank You" reminded Epi of the other half of the saying from

---

6   Uncle
7   Grandpa
8   Boys, sons; a term of endearment for young men

<u>G'Morning, G'Night"</u> [9]…Good night, don't forget to look up from your work & let life in. It makes your work better." He smiled to himself and turned to his brother, his work partner. They gave each other a pat on the back and enjoyed the last song even more.

By the end of the night the boys had danced themselves to sleep. Boni's mom called Pop to come pick up the working boys.

A few minutes later, Pop showed up. He walked in and greeted Dolores and wished the sleepy Boni a "Happy Birthday." He walked over to the chairs on the back patio. As he picked up the sleeping Milo, he woke Epi. "Mijo, come on. I came to give you a ride home." The three headed to the door, "You two had fun, I see."

Epi wiped the sleep from his eyes. "Yeah Pop. Both of us."

They both said their 'good nights' and 'thank yous' to Boni and her mom before they walked out to Pop's truck.

"Pop?" asked Epi, strolling slowly beside him.

"Yes mijo?"

"Why do you carry Milo and I have to walk?"

Pop answered, without a thought, "Well Panzón, Milo is little and... um... Mijo, you're big."

"Oh," as he thought to himself, "That's pretty simple logic."

---

9   Miranda, Lin-Manuel. *G'Morning, G'Night!: Little Pep Talks for Me & You.* Random House Publishing House, 2018.

9

Potluck Unlucky

Wolf Scouts was something Epi couldn't wait to be involved in. This was the year he was old enough to join. Epi looked forward to the Saturday meetings with the rest of the Pack of scouts. He knew at each meeting they would learn and practice all the cool skills from their Wolf Scout handbook. The more they practiced the closer they got to earning badges. Exciting!

On that morning at home Ma had tried for the past 30 minutes to get Epi ready. He kept fidgeting and Ma was getting frustrated.

"Panzón, stop moving," she said, "I need to finish fixing the sleeves on your shirt. You know we had to get a larger shirt for you, *verdad*? [1] Well, the sleeves are too long, so let me fix them."

---

1   True?

Epi was nicknamed *El Panzón*, the chubby kid, by his family for a reason.

Still moving around, Epi told his Ma, "But I have to go meet the guys at Paco's. Boni is already there since her mom dropped her off. I don't want to be late." Epi began to pull away.

"Epifanio," Ma raised her voice.

Epi knew he was in trouble when Ma used his full name. He stopped moving immediately.

"OK, Panzóncito, I am almost done," Ma said, in a calmer tone. She pulled tight the thread then cut it by biting it. "There."

Epi turned and looked into mom's big mirror. He saw the green kerchief with all his Pack patches, each in their correct place according to the manual. With Ma's work complete, Epi buttoned his hemmed sleeves and pressed his shirt front down. He ran his thumb just inside the waist of his pants to be sure his uniform top was tucked in neatly. It was. "Yes, I'm a Wolf Scout."

Epi was extremely happy when he reached the age to join the Wolf Scouts Pack 65. Other classmates had joined before, but this year he and his closest friends—Boni, Cuatro and Cinco, and little Travi—were now all old enough.

Epi walked from Ma's room down the hall. As he passed the family portrait that hung there, he noticed his reflection in the glass. He stood there for a moment and once again admired his new uniform, kerchief and kerchief holder with the Wolf on it. And, of course, with his Wolf Scouts hat, he was set.

Epi continued through the living room and toward the back door. He was about to leave when his Ma told him to wait for her to get the camera. He normally protested pictures, but she had already used his full name once, so he didn't dare. She lined him up against the wall in the kitchen and took what seemed like a hundred pictures.

When she was done, Epi said goodbye and got on his bike. His den meeting was at Ronny's house. Ronny's mom, Mrs. Sarah, was the Den Leader. That made it even better since he knew her and where they lived.

As Epi rode past Travi's house, he whistled for him. Travi was out the back door and on his bike before Epi had to whistle twice. If there was anything Epi learned well from his Pop was whistling.

After Travi caught up with Epi, they rode together towards Paco's Tacos taco truck to pick up Cuatro and Cinco. The twins lived near them, but Epi knew on Saturday mornings they were both at the taco truck helping their dad.

When they arrived, Epi noticed Travi's uniform was big on him. "What happened to your shirt Travi?" asked Epi, "It's huge on you."

"I don't know," said Travi with a puzzled look on his face.

From the back door of the taco truck, Cuatro, dressed in his own crisp new Wolf Scout uniform, walked out and greeted his friends. "Hey Epi! Hey Tra…" he stopped, looked at Travi, then let out a laugh, "Whoa Travi! Now I know what happened. Cinco! Come here."

Cinco, who was still in the taco truck, yelled back, "No!"

Cuatro, snapped back, "Come here. I found the answer to your problem."

With reluctance in his voice, Cinco finally said, "OK" and slowly walked out of the truck.

The guys quickly noticed Cinco was squished into the smallest of uniform shirts. Cinco was not as well-fed of a kid as Epi, but this shirt was by far too small for him.

As Cinco walked closer to the group, he saw Travi and Travi saw him. At that same moment, the looks on their faces were mirrored. Their expressions shouted: "How?" "Why?" and "That's MY shirt."

Epi turned to Cuatro and quietly asked him, "What happened?"

Cuatro explained, "We all ordered our shirts from the Scout Store downtown and we went together to pick them up. Our names were on the bags, but you know how Travi likes to play around. He and Cinco were in the backseat play fighting, hitting each other with the bags until everything came flying out. Mami finally told them to stop, so they did. I guess the shirts got mixed up in all the fun.

"Oh, that makes sense," Epi nodded.

Cuatro continued, "You know how Cinco is: he likes everything nice and neat. He was sure he wasn't going today because of the mix up. My mom said 'Mijo, you signed up, you bought the uniform, you are going. We will fix it later' so here he is." He gave his brother a huge grin.

Cinco rolled his eyes at Cuatro. Travi and Cinco exchanged shirts, both feeling much better as they buttoned up and fixed their kerchiefs.

Epi looked down at his watch. He exclaimed, "Hey guys! We have to go! It's almost time." They all jumped on their bikes. Cuatro and Cinco said "Goodbye" to their dad and rode off.

They rode through the neighborhood as fast as they could. They knew their next obstacle was The Bridge. The walking/riding bridge that took them over the freeway was always a struggle for the cycling crew of Epi and his friends.

The four of them each made their efforts up the front side. Cinco made it the farthest, until he too had to walk the rest of the way up. Once all four boys arrived at the top, and Epi took his customary breather, it was time for the fun. Each boy made a special brake skid mark as they exited The Bridge.

They passed the school then rode through City Heights Shopping Center. Epi didn't know which was more tempting—the Gotta Read bookshop or the Big Fat Donut Shop. Still, he knew he was off to a den meeting so that was more important.

"I'll get something on the way back," he thought with a smile. As he looked back, he noticed Cinco having to keep Cuatro and Travi from stopping at Save-Much Market where video games were. Epi could see the disappointment on both Travi and Cuatro's faces.

The boys all arrived on time for their first Den meeting. Epi, Travi and the twins all fixed their kerchiefs and their hats. They made sure their shirts were tucked in because a Wolf Scout was always ready. They knocked on the door. Ronny greeted them and invited them in. Boni was standing behind him. Both Ronny and she saluted them with the Wolf Scout salute then they all did a howl.

They walked into the living room where a circle of chairs had been set up. Mrs. Sarah wore her yellow Pack Leader shirt, short-sleeved with the same Pack 65 patches and Wolf Scout insignia as the boys. Her hat was different. It looked more like a field explorer hat, and right in front it read: PACK LEADER.

Mrs. Sarah saluted them and opened the meeting by asking the question: "Has the Pack assembled?" to which all the scouts responded with loud voices, "YES, PACK LEADER!" Everyone present, including Mrs. Sarah, howled!

The Pack meeting consisted of roll call to make sure everyone was there, then announcements for the coming week. Epi was excited at the fact that, starting next week, each meeting would have a potluck. Every Wolf Scout would need to bring something to eat and share.

"Food AND being a Wolf Scout every Saturday?! What a bonus!" thought Epi, "If this is a potluck then that means they will probably order pizza and the rest of us will just bring chips and drinks. That's how they do it at school. Yeah, that would be it."

For the remainder of the meeting the kids learned how to tie rope knots and how to pitch a tent with just rope, a blanket, and some wooden stakes.

The following week when it came time to take something for the potluck, Epi asked his mom to buy a big bag of chips.

Ma asked, "You don't want me to make something like a meal?"

Epi answered, "No, Ma. They're going to get pizza and we're just supposed to bring, like drinks or chips or desserts."

Ma said, "Is that what your Pack leader said?"

Epi quickly said, "Yes" because that's what Epi assumed. He didn't notice the questioning look on his Ma's face.

That Saturday morning, Ma gave him the big bag of potato chips he had asked for. Epi said "Goodbye, Ma. I will see you in a little while."

Ma waved at him but still wondered whether he was correct. He didn't give her time to ask him again as he rode off. She thought he would find out soon enough. Ma watched as he rode around the corner toward his meeting.

Epi rode his bike fast and finally caught up with the rest of the crew, who were waiting for him at Paco's Tacos. When he saw them, he noticed what they were carrying. He felt as if he was right when he saw Travi struggling riding with two large bottles of soda in a grocery bag hanging from his handlebars. Boni, had a SuperSeal container with a sealed lid, she said was filled with blueberry muffins her mom made. However, he grew a little doubtful when he saw Cuatro and Cinco each with a carry-all bag, with "Paco's Tacos" written on the side.

He asked them, "What do you guys have?"

Cinco said, "My dad made a batch of tacos to take. I am carrying that and Cuatro has the salsa and stuff that goes with it in his bag."

Epi really liked when the twins' dad, Paco, made food, but he was concerned that only one bag had tacos in it. If that was true, that bag wasn't very big.

"How many tacos did they bring?" Epi wondered. He really hoped there would be more food there than just his chips, the drinks that Travi had, and that one bag of tacos.

When they knocked on the door, Ronny again greeted them and then saluted them with the Wolf howl. He asked them to take the food over to the dinner table where everything was being set up. Epi noticed a large number of desserts, a few bags of chips, bottles of soda and now the bag of tacos. He asked himself, "Where is the pizza?" He told himself that it would be delivered later so it would be nice and hot.

He went into the living room, and they started the meeting. Today they were going to work on identifying animal tracks. As the afternoon went on, Epi felt his stomach growling. He still hadn't heard the doorbell for the pizza delivery guy.

As soon as Mrs. Sarah had the scouts do their final Wolf salute, Epi knew it was time for lunch. Epi helped clean up the living room and put the chairs away. He was thinking that the pizza must be in the kitchen, and he couldn't wait to make sure he got a nice warm slice. He got to the table and lined up behind the others. He noticed there was nothing new except a big bowl at the end.

"That doesn't look like a pizza to me," he told himself.

Standing behind his friends, what he thought earlier came true: that small bag of tacos wasn't going to last for long. So, with two muffins, a handful of chips and a cup of soda Epi arrived at a lonely, empty bag of tacos. As to the mysterious big bowl at the end of the table, when Epi looked inside, he realized it wasn't a bowl of fried chicken or hot dogs but a large portion of fruit salad.

Epi's heart sunk into his empty stomach. He was not a salad guy, much less a fruit salad guy. He walked away and sat down near his friends in the backyard. He finished off his plate, but he knew he was going to be super hungry before he got home.

On the ride home he trailed behind the rest of the guys, still feeling hunger pangs. He knew Ma would have something to eat, but he'd also have to face telling her that she was right.

"Anyways," he said, as a better idea came to mind, "I can ask her to make me something for next week, then I'll know there will be some good stuff there."

This thought made him a little happier and a little less hungry. He started to catch up with the gang feeling more energetic knowing next week would be better. Of course, in his current condition, The Bridge was going to be that much harder to get over.

On Thursday. Epi gave his Ma a reminder about the potluck on Saturday for his Pack meeting.

"Maybe she'll make some taquitos or a large pan of enchiladas," he told himself, "I don't know how I'm gonna get it there but if I have to walk, I'll do it."

Epi was excited about the prospect of walking into his Pack meeting with a nice pan of his Ma's enchiladas.

After Epi reminded Ma over dinner, she gave him a look that made him confused. It was a combination of sadness and hesitation. She said, "Ay Panzón. I can't make you something for Saturday. Mijo, you know ever since I began selling SuperSeal kitchen products, I have been very busy. All my comadres[2] love them. This Friday and Saturday I have two SuperSeal parties to be at."

Epi could not believe what he was hearing. What was he going to do? He walked out of the kitchen and down the hall.

His next thought was, "Well maybe Paola can make them for him." He knew to ask his sister for anything meant to be as nice and courteous as possible.

He knocked on her bedroom door softly. No answer. Paola was forever listening to her favorite music loudly. Epi knocked a little louder then heard the music soften and Paola opened the door. Epi asked her but her answer came very quickly.

"No, Epi. I can't," said Paola, "I have to work on Friday night and I'm opening the movie theater on Saturday, so I don't have time to be making you anything for your little meeting."

"But, but…" said Epi, "I mean there's nothing to eat there."

Paola repeated herself, "I can't Epi. Make something yourself if you're so worried about it," and with that she closed her door and turned up her music again.

"Make something myself? Really?" Epi walked down the hall to his room.

Epi's mind was in a frenzy trying to figure out how to get food that he could actually eat to his Pack meeting. He was lying on his top bunk bed when Milo came into their room. He rushed in, belly-sliding on their little rug, as if he had just crossed another goal line. He looked up to see his brother's reaction—nothing.

---

2   Comadre= close friend; many times, godmother to friend's child

"Hey Epi! What's going on?" asked Milo.

No answer.

Milo could just see Epi's feet swinging side to side, but he was making no sound. Milo finally decided to climb up the side of the bunk beds and perch himself at the top of their tall dresser.

Sitting eye to eye with Epi, Milo tapped him on the shoulder and said "What is wrong, dude?"

Epi turned slowly to his brother and with the saddest eyes, said, "I am going to starve to death this Saturday."

Milo stared at Epi with a combination of shock and laughter. "What?!" he asked, "Don't you have your Pack meetings on Saturdays?"

Epi answered "Yes, that's why!"

Now even more confused, Milo leaned in toward his brother and asked Epi to explain.

"Look, we're having potlucks now for lunch at my Pack meetings. The last time I assumed that Mrs. Sarah, was going to order pizza. I took only a bag of chips. I think the other guys thought so too. When I got there, there was no big food. There were only a lot of desserts, some soda and a very funky looking fruit salad." Epi sighed remembering the rumbling in his tummy that day.

"Wow," said Milo, "What's up with that?"

"I don't know," said Epi, "but I thought I had the answer when I asked Ma to make me some food that I could take. That was the solution to my problem, but then Ma told me today that she can't. She is doing Super Seal parties on Friday night and Saturday."

"What about Paola?" said Milo.

Epi replied quickly, "I asked her, but she said she can't either. She's working on Friday and Saturday."

"Oh dude. That's rough," lamented Milo, "but why don't we just make them ourselves?"

At once, it felt like a light bulb went on. Epi sort of whispered out loud, "Why don't I just make it myself?" He continued to think, "I've seen Ma make enchiladas my whole life. I am pretty sure I could do it. Yeah! I could do it."

While Epi's eyes rolled back and forth and back and forth in deep thought, Milo just sat silently waiting.

Epi began his proposal, "Hey Milo! You wanna help me make a whole batch of enchiladas?!"

Milo put his hand to his chin, rubbing it in contemplation.

"I'll share some with you," added Epi.

Epi had Milo at 'share some.' He shook Epi's hand vigorously. Milo jumped on Epi's top bunk, and asked, "When do we start?"

The boys spent the better part of the late morning working out their plan.

The next day after school the two boys began their research for the recipe for making enchiladas. First, they rode their bikes to Save-Much Mart. There was a magazine section that had cooking magazines, like *Chez Fantastique*. They spent an hour skimming through them all, but none had what they were looking for.

Next, they left their bikes locked near Save-Much and walked across the parking lot to Gotta Read bookshop. They had to believe the cookbooks there would have something. When they walked in Doyle, the Bookshop clerk, greeted them. Doyle was a young man in his twenties. His older sisters were the local librarians in the area, while he ran the family bookshop. Doyle always wore a beret, an untucked dress shirt with a vest, and his horn-rimmed glasses. Epi was sure this was what an author looked like.

"Hello Boys! We received some new comic books this week. Would you like me to show you?" asked Doyle.

"No, thank you," answered Milo, "We are on a different mission today. Where are the cookbooks, please?" Doyle pointed to the two tall bookshelves in the rear corner of the shop. The boys thanked him and walked over, leaving Doyle to take off his beret and scratch his head. He shrugged his shoulder and went back to the journal he had been writing in.

Epi and Milo looked up at the two shelves. They each took a shelf and sat down with their first cookbook to review. Milo found one that read "Recipes for Kids," but it was filled with sandwiches, sweet treats and cutesy snacks. "Nope," he told himself and put it back, grabbing another to look at. Epi had also begun skimming his first choice. This one was written by a famous TV chef. Nothing.

The boys spent the next two hours choosing cookbooks, rejecting them and choosing another. They were growing frustrated with this research project. Epi was on his last choice. He went through each section: Meats, Baking, Dinners, etc. He stopped suddenly and shouted to Milo, "LOOK! I found a recipe for enchiladas." Milo spun around and scooted over to him. He had exhausted his shelf and was sitting, leaning against the book racks near him. They both looked through the prized recipe. Unfortunately, their faces soured the more they read. None of the ingredients resembled anything Ma used. Even the large picture next to the printed instructions looked nothing like what they've enjoyed eating from their Ma.

"We will never find it in these books," said Epi, which was a hard realization for him. He had always found amazing ideas and How-To's in the books he read. Epi looked at Milo who returned the same sad look, when in an instant, Milo's face changed to one of excitement.

"EPI! We could get the recipe from Ma, maybe even Paola! They make enchiladas all the time."

Epi eyed his little brother with doubt, "They're not going to tell us. They will figure out what we're doing."

"No, they won't," explained Milo, "We will watch them cook then find ways to sneak in the right questions, specifically about cooking enchiladas. Get it?"

"I think so," Epi responded with an expression that showed he was beginning to understand his brother's plan. Saying goodbye to Doyle, the boys left the shop and walked back to their bicycles. Before they rode home, the brothers decided they would begin their Top Secret observations of Ma and Paola when they got home.

Milo and Epi got home and put their bikes away before going in. They were sure that between Paola and Ma everything that they would need to know to make enchiladas was there. The trick was how to frame their questions as if they were simply being curious. Throughout the rest of the day, they both tried very hard not to let on what their plan was. Between Ma and Paola, the boys believed their sister was getting suspicious of their questioning. Nevertheless, they kept going.

Once they had the recipe Epi went through the pantry to make sure they had all the ingredients. The good thing was that Ma was very meticulous when it came to grocery shopping. She would find the best deals, take her time to find the best quality items, and always ensure they had a full pantry. Epi found everything they would need for their first cooking endeavor.

Saturday morning came quick enough. The boys had a restless sleep the night before, so much so they were up early enough to hear Pop leave for work. They stayed in bed and got up at their normal time—around 9am—so as not to draw any suspicion. They made their regular breakfast of milk with breakfast cereal, and orange juice, then went to watch their Saturday morning cartoons, as usual. From their perch on the couch, they saw Ma and Paola get themselves ready for the day.

Ma left first to go to her Super Seal party. Both Epi and Milo carried her sample bag and other goodies to the car around 10 am. They waved goodbye and went back inside to wait for Paola to leave a little bit before 11 am. She would be trickier. Like many big sisters, Paola always kept a watchful eye on her little brothers.

When Paola walked into the living room to say goodbye to the boys, she noticed both of their cereal bowls were still full. "What's going on? You both are usually done and gone with your cereal by the time your second show comes on?" asked Paola with a suspicious tone, "What are you guys plotting this time?" She stood over them.

"Man, Pao-Pao, you are always so suspicious of us," said Milo, "We just got into our cartoons and didn't finish. Right Epi?"

Epi nodded, his mouth full of cereal, trying to finish the bowl.

Paola crossed her arms and stared at them both, "Really?"

Epi was nervous, but Milo stayed in it with her. He softened his voice with her and said, "Maybe you're just tired from staying up late on the phone…with Reuben."

Paola's mouth dropped. Epi had frozen mid-spoonful.

"Whatever," she said abruptly, "Don't break anything," and left for work.

Epi was impressed with his little brother. "When were you up to hear all that?" he asked.

"I wasn't. Her bed is against our wall, and she talks on the phone in bed at night sometimes. I guessed at the name, though." explained Milo. They both laughed and Epi smacked Milo on the back in triumph.

With everyone gone, Epi and Milo looked at each other as if they were planning the caper of the century. Epi said to Milo, "OK we have two hours to get everything done and packed so we can take it to my Pack meeting."

Milo asked, "What do you mean 'WE take it?' "

Epi replied, "If you want your portion then you're gonna have to help me get it there."

Milo thought about it for a minute and said "OK. Where do we start?"

The new cooking partners headed to the kitchen. They rinsed out their cereal bowls and put the cereal and milk away.

Epi said, "According to what Ma said, you have to soft fry the corn tortillas then pile them on a plate.

Milo said, "Yeah that's what Paola said too, but Epi we've never cooked anything before."

The boys looked at each other. They realized this fact was something they should have contemplated before this moment. Still, at the same time they both knew there was no turning back now.

Epi said, "I see Ma using tongs to fry the tortillas. Since this is my first time doing it, I figured, to be safe, we can use Pop's tongs from his barbecue set. You know, the long ones."

Milo nodded his head in agreement then went into the storage closet to get them. Epi poured the oil into a pan and very carefully turned on the flame. A sigh of relief when it came on and Epi figured, "OK we can do this." He took out the enchilada sauce that Ma would buy from the Little Mexican food store.

Milo's job was to shred the cheese. He got the block of cheese and cheese grater. He started shredding then saw Ma's new food processor. It was one of the first things she bought with her SuperSeal money. He looked at it and thought this would make his job much easier.

To himself, Milo thought, "OK. Ma cut the block into smaller chunks and puts it into this opening." He did it carefully. "Then she turns it on." Click. Whirrrrrrr! PHOOM!

What Milo neglected to do was to use the Pusher to help him move the cheese down. The Pusher was a large plastic block that fit directly into the opening in order to help keep the items inside. When Milo put in his first square of cheese and turned on the machine, it launched out of the opening like a small cheddar rocket. It flew over Epi's head. Over the table. Over the ceiling fan. Eventually it landed on a high shelf, barely missing one of Ma's decorations.

Epi turned to Milo, "What are you doing?!"

"I'm shredding the cheese."

"Yeah, but what was that?" as he pointed to the block of cheese now hiding behind a ceramic rooster on the shelf.

Milo looked then turned back to the job. "I got this. I got it." He cut a piece from the block and slowly using the pusher, he started shredding the cheese.

Epi shook his finger at him, which made some sauce fly, and said "Quit playing. We don't have much time."

Milo with his back to him, waved him off.

Milo did much better grating the cheese. However, he was in kind of a hurry now. Each time he emptied the food processor's container into the large bowl, he spilled a little more cheese all over the counter.

Once he filled up the bowl, he stopped and brought the cheese to Epi who had a nice pile of corn tortillas ready.

"Now the next step," said Epi, "I will dip each tortilla into the enchilada sauce then we will roll them."

Milo let out a sigh because he knew the tortillas were hot and the sauce was hot. "But I told him I'd help him," he said to himself.

He brought over his stepping stool and went near the counter next to the stove. Epi dipped each tortilla into the sauce and placed them into the rectangular baking pan. Milo laid cheese down the center of each tortilla and tried to roll them. He wasn't very successful at keeping them rolled but he tried. He was right. The tortillas were hot. This slowed him down.

Epi saw his brother struggling with keeping the tortillas in their rolled form. He decided to scoot over and help him roll. He knew they were running out of time, at this point. As it happened every time the boys would roll an enchilada it would unroll itself.

They couldn't figure out how to keep them together when suddenly Epi said, "How about you roll one then I roll one and I put mine on top of yours to see if that will keep them together?"

Milo agreed, "We might as well. We weren't doing that good before."

He rolled two tortillas and held them there in place while Epi rolled two more and placed them on top. They let go and "BOOM!" They stayed! The boys High Five'd each other, which was not the best idea since their hands were full of sauce. Red bubbles splashed practically everywhere. They paused for a moment, but they were happy with themselves, so they began their process again.

Milo would roll two and put them in. Epi would roll two and put his on top. They continued this way until they filled up their baking pan full of enchiladas. Epi got a spoon and poured a little bit more sauce all over the top. He carefully used his potholder to put the pan into the oven that he had warming up.

Epi set the timer then told his brother, "We really need to clean up."

While their dish was warming in the oven, the boys wiped down the counter with wet towels and cleanser. They also had to wash out all the pots and pans and utensils.

"Orale!" exclaimed Epi, "This is a lot of work. I don't know if I could be a chef if you have to do all this AND clean."

Milo said, "I know what you mean. I see Ma doing this all the time, too, and without any recipes or cookbooks. You know what? After today, I'm not sure we could be a mom." They both laughed, but they did have a newfound respect for all the work Ma did for them, and the cooking knowledge she had.

When the timer went off, they had just finished the dishes. Epi went over again with his potholder to open up the oven and review their masterpiece. Unfortunately, when he pulled out the pan, their enchiladas did not look anything like what they looked like when they went in. It would seem all of their enchiladas unrolled and that they were all over the baking pan. He figured as the cheese melted and the tortillas cooked a little more, everything spread out.

Epi put the pan on top of the stove. He turned off everything and just sat in a chair at the table. Milo, too, was disappointed and sat down next to him.

He whispered to Epi, "They don't look like enchiladas to me, Epi."

Epi sadly nodded his head.

At that moment, the boys both caught something fragrant and familiar in the air. The boys sniffed the air and looked at each other.

"Something smells reeeeally good," they exclaimed. Both boys had enormous smiles on their faces.

In unison, they rose from their seats and looked at their creation. They focused their noses on the pan.

Milo was the first to react. "Wow! Whatever those are, they really smell good."

Epi agreed with him, "Let's try 'em!"

Epi and Milo each got a fork and went to two different corners of the pan. They cut a piece out of the cheesy dish and looked at each other. The moment they put their forks in their mouths and savored the taste, Epi and Milo realized they had used the right ingredients, and they had followed the directions correctly! Even though their enchiladas didn't stay together, the dish had come out almost perfect.

Milo, smacked his lips, asked, "Well, what are we going to call it? I mean they're gonna ask what it is."

"I don't know," answered Epi, "An Enchilada...pie?"

Milo agreed excitedly, "Yeah, that sounds right. It does kind of look like a pie, or a cake. No, A pie sounds good. Enchilada Pie!"

The boys finished cleaning up. They wrapped their Enchilada Pie with foil. Epi figured he would tie his wagon to the back of his bike and make sure that the pan didn't move. Milo followed him all the way to the Pack meeting. They helped each other get over The Bridge and carefully navigated through the shopping center. The brothers were so focused on their mission that Epi didn't even glance at Gotta Read bookshop or Big Fat Donut Shop, and Milo didn't flinch when he saw the door open to Save-Much Mart. They were determined to get to their destination.

When they got to Ronny's house, Epi told him that he needed to look after his brother today and that's why Milo was there. He also said they had brought food for the potluck. Mrs. Sarah welcomed Milo and showed Epi where to place his dish.

Mrs. Sarah asked Epi, "What did you bring to share?"

Epi proudly but still somewhat nervously, answered, "An Enchilada Pie. Me and Milo made it." He patted Milo's shoulder. Milo smiled and slightly elbowed his brother in the side.

Mrs. Sarah was impressed and told Epi, "I will warm it up for you. The troop is in the living room."

Both boys joined in the Pack meeting. Today they all had fun using a map to identify different national parks. When it came time for lunch, Epi and Milo were suddenly nervous. They both wondered if everybody would like what they had come up with. They knew they liked it, but it did not look like regular enchiladas. After Mrs. Sarah took it out of the oven and everyone took a piece for their lunch, it didn't take long for them to get their answer.

"Oh, this is so good!" exclaimed Travi.

"Wow!" said Cinco, "This is great."

Boni stated, as a matter of fact, "I've never seen your mom make them like this, but they are awesome!"

"Yeah, you can get as big or as small a piece of enchilada as you want from this thing," explained Ronny.

Cuatro didn't say anything. He just kept eating it and serving himself more.

Milo and Epi were happy that their friends enjoyed their food. Epi hadn't even sat down or served himself yet. He was just soaking up the satisfaction his troop had with each bite.

He told Milo, "This must be what Ma feels like when we eat up all her food. Maybe that's why she doesn't sit down: she just likes watching us enjoy it."

"Yeah," agreed Milo, as he finished a bite, "But I still couldn't be a 'mom.'"

Epi nodded. He took a plate and finally served himself. "Funny, I think I am full already."

After all the Wolf Scouts pitched in and cleaned up, everyone howled their goodbyes and left for home. Epi and Milo were surprised when they saw that their Enchilada Pie was almost gone.

"I guessed they liked it," Epi told Milo.

"You think?" Milo responded and laughed out loud.

The boys rode home but decided to walk the rest of the way after The Bridge. As the boys turned the last corner, they noticed everyone was home. Pop's truck, Ma's station wagon, and Paola's little "putt-putt" car, the boys called it, were all in their long driveway. A chill came over the boys.

"Did we clean up enough?" Epi asked his brother.

"For sure, we did. Then we put everything in the dishwasher," Milo answered.

"But we were supposed to be home in time to put it all away."

"Meh, Ma doesn't use the dishwasher so we will get in there and put them away when she's not looking. We're good," Milo said with confidence.

Epi was still a little worried but as they walked up the driveway to the back door, he calmed down. "We did clean up. They won't know," he thought. They left the pan in the wagon and went in.

As soon as they opened the door, they noticed something. Sniff, sniff. The beautiful smell of enchiladas was still evident. The more they walked in the more they could smell the delicious aroma - that and a subtle smell of cleanser from their cleaning towels.

They turned toward the full view of the kitchen and the boys' eyes widened. There standing near the stove was Ma, Pop, and Paola.

Epi gave a jittery "Hello."

Milo shouted his normal, "Hey everybody! What's going on?"

Ma and Pop, and Paola, too, all gave them a serious stare. Epi's eyes lowered a bit, but Milo still tried to act as if nothing had happened.

"Ma! Mmmmm...it smells great in here. Did you start cleaning already? I can smell that fresh pine scent." he said, smiling.

"Emiliano?"

"Yes?"

"Epifanio?"

"Y-y-yes, Ma?"

"What is this and how did it get on the shelf?" asked Ma. She nudged Paola to reveal a small chunk of cheddar cheese.

The boys stood stunned. They looked at one another and realized they hadn't removed it from the shelf where it landed.

Milo began, "Well, Ma, Pop, you see this mouse…"

Pop frowned directly at Milo.

Epi put his hand on Milo's shoulder and interrupted, "No, we cooked today. We cooked enchiladas for my Pack meeting."

Pop, Ma and Paola all gasped.

Epi went on to explain that he was afraid of going hungry again at his meeting. He mentioned that he had asked Ma and Paola to cook something for him, but they couldn't. He understood why but it still meant he would starve. Pop gave a slight laugh. Ma elbowed him. Epi continued by saying after Paola said she had to work, she told him to make something himself.

Paola dropped her jaw and turned to Ma to explain. Ma motioned for her to wait. Paola glared back at Epi. Funny enough, Milo gestured to her like he had a phone in his hand. She mouthed "Whatever."

Epi described how the boys had learned the recipe from Ma, checked for all ingredients, carefully cooked everything, and assembled the enchiladas.

"OK," Ma said, "but how did it turn out? I mean you served it to other people. I hope it wasn't bad."

Milo ran to the pan in the wagon and brought in the leftovers wrapped in foil. He removed the foil and put it on a plate. After a few seconds in the microwave, he offered it to Ma, Pop, and Paola to try it. To their great surprise, it tasted good. Very Good! They ate the rest on the plate quickly and turned back to the boys.

Still with a stern look on her face, Ma began, "They weren't bad, mijo. What happened to their shape though?"

Epi explained the whole unraveling process.

Ma asked, "What did you tell your friends they were then? I am sure they could tell that they didn't look like enchiladas."

Milo interjected, "We called it an Enchilada Pie!"

Ma relaxed her shoulders from her upset mood and said, "Panzón, Milo, it was wrong for you to try this alone—using the stove, the can opener, the food processor, and everything else." She paused to make sure the boys are listening. They were. "Also, food is very special. If you don't make it right, someone could have gotten sick. Finally, you know your papa and I don't approve of you hiding the truth."

Both brothers hung their heads. They knew what she was saying was right.

"Still, I see why you did this," she continued, "I am sorry I could not make anything for you. Next time, I will make something ahead of time and put it in the fridge for you." Epi smiled slightly. "And you have shown me that you both are old enough to start to learn how to cook. Your Pop and I will start to teach you both some skills in the kitchen - maybe for the BBQ too."

Epi and Milo were beaming. They never thought it would turn out this well for them—learning to cook their favorite and BBQing, too! They both walked toward the back door to put away their bikes.

"Wait a minute!" Ma said, as if interrupting a celebration, "Your punishment will be no TV, riding bikes or playing outside this weekend, and to wash all the dirty dishes."

"Yes, Ma," said the boys in unison.

"Starting now," said Pop, as he walked toward them.

"What do you mean?" asked Epi.

"Yeah, we washed them all before we left," added Milo.

At that moment, Pop opened the dishwasher and revealed the full racks of dirty pans, pots, and utensils.

"What?" exclaimed Epi, "I turned it on right when we left. What happened?"

Pop smiled and explained, "Your Ma never uses the dishwasher. I unplugged it a long time ago."

A huge sigh and the boys looked at each other. "We should have known that."

Epi and Milo walked over to begin washing the dishes. As Milo moved his stepping stool toward the sink, he remembered something.

"How did you know about the cheese?" he asked.

Ma and Pop laughed. Paola shrugged her shoulders at her parents as if to say, "Why are you laughing?"

"It fell on your sister's head after she plopped down in the chair near it. She must have knocked it loose," explained Pop, still chuckling.

The boys sheepishly looked over at their sister. They couldn't help but smile, too, which made her grit her teeth at them. They knew she would be mad at them for a while, but she had to admit it was funny.

As she walked out of the kitchen, Ma said, "That reminds me, you need to wash my rooster statue, too."

10

"W-I-N" spells Win

With the coming of spring, the mood in class was changing. It was the Great School Spelling Bee time again. The Hillside Elementary School spelling bee was a big thing. Ribbons, trophies, but more than that, the winner had bragging rights for the year!

As the spelling bee neared, Epi was focusing more and more on his plan for beating William. Unfortunately, it was consuming much of his time with his friends.

Sitting on the top bunk in his room at home, Epi was digging into his dictionary. He heard Milo in the hallway.

As he thumped against the wall, Milo jumped, caught his football, shuffled his feet, then said, "Oh yeah. Whose arm is like McNabb? Who jukes like McCoy? Catches like D.J.? Milo, Milo, Milo!"

Milo ran toward the door to the bedroom. He stopped just short of entering. With toes on the edge, he tossed the ball up and caught it as he fell into the room. THUMP!

Finally fed up with Milo's noisemaking, Epi yelled, "Milo!"

Milo responded, "I know, right? Mighty Milo does it again." He spiked his football on the floor so hard it bounced high and landed on Epi's open book. The book nearly dropped out of his hands.

Epi, in frustration, told him, "¡Ya Milo! I'm trying to study. Go play outside."

"No, Ma told me to come see what you're doing." He spun his football on the floor of their room and practiced his touchdown dance—something between a disco turn and a moonwalk.

"I'm studying! OK? You know now. Go away!" Epi closed his eyes and tried to memorize the last words he read.

"Ma's going to come over here. You know what she's going to tell you," Milo recited, in his best impression of his Ma's voice, "¡Ay Panzón! Why? Why are you inside? Mijo, you need to go outside and run around."

Epi contemplated jumping down and to grab his brother as he normally would do, but instead just rolled his eyes and explained, "I know but this year I'm WINNING the school spelling bee."

Milo jabbed back at Epi, "Really? So, William isn't there anymore?" He giggled, then stopped suddenly. Epi gave Milo that Big Brother look that meant something was about to happen; something Milo probably would not like. Milo took his football and walked out of the room slowly, backwards.

At school, Ms. Nikols' class, which Epi and the gang were in, had an ongoing rivalry with the students in Mr. Clayton's class. They were in the same grade and evenly matched in many ways. On this day, the kids were organizing a kickball game at recess.

Cinco was captain for Ms. Nikols' class. He got to choose the team. Timmy from Mr. Clayton's class would choose the other.

Cuatro asked Milo, "Where's Epi?" Epi was a key player on their team.

Milo rolled his eyes and answered, "Where else has he been every recess this week?—The Library studying for the spelling bee."

Cuatro gave a slight smile. He knew Milo was right.

After picking the first five players on their teams, the team captains each had one spot left to fill. Believing Epi would have arrived by now, Cinco said, "I choose Epi." Everyone looked around then centered on Milo. Milo shrugged his shoulders and pointed at the library.

Timmy said, "You will have to play with one player down, I guess." He laughed then said, "My last player will be William."

They all looked around again then Jenn whispered in Timmy's ear and pointed at the library. Cinco and the gang laughed. The kids decided to play anyway.

The school library wasn't huge, but the students loved it. There were picture books for the Pre-K and Kindergarten kids, small children's books for beginning readers, and chapter books for the older, advanced readers. Its Reference section was what was in demand today, especially by Epi.

At the table near the Reference section, Epi could be found behind a stack of dictionaries. He was crossing off words on the given spelling bee study list. He recited the spelling for "peninsula," and felt excitement at seeing he did it correctly. That was ten words in a row today. He flipped through the list, and thought, "I only have three pages to go over again."

Epi was feeling more confident today. He had been in the library every recess and every lunch so far this week. He hadn't seen William in there. "I must be studying more than him this time."

The bell rang and Epi started to move the dictionaries off his table. "I will study tonight then maybe I can be back to play at recess tomorrow," he thought, then he suddenly saw William come out of one of the library study rooms.

William walked over to the librarian, Mrs. Agatha. She was an older woman, grey-haired neatly in a bun behind her head. Her sweater lay over her shoulders fastened with one button at the top. Her pale-yellow blouse and dress were always kept as neat as she kept the library itself. Books were a part of her life. Her two younger sisters, Beatrix and Charlotte, were also local librarians, and the youngest, their brother Doyle, worked at the Gotta Read Bookshop. Epi had heard the four siblings were all named for famous authors.

William greeted Mrs. Agatha and handed her his book.

"Hello. I see you finished another study session. Will you be back tomorrow?" she asked.

William shook his head, and said, "No, I am done. I finished the list three times already," with a big smile. As he left, he turned and saw Epi. They locked eyes.

Epi broke the stare and said to himself in a whisper, "He's gone through the list THREE times, then I will work even harder. Now that he thinks he is done; I will show him that I am not."

When Epi looked back, William was out the door. Epi gritted his teeth, even more determined to win the spelling bee.

After another intense day of studying, Epi and family were all at home for family dinner. In this home, dinner time meant the smell of Ma's amazing food filled the house. Ma was wrapping up cooking, while Paola made the taco shells. Dinner time also meant that the entire family sat down together.

Pop was home already from work and Milo handled the "Welcome Home" duties for their father alone. Pop asked Milo where his brother was, and Milo motioned to the room. His dad nodded. He got up and walked into the kitchen to greet Ma and Paola. They both gave him a kiss and asked about his day.

After a few more minutes, all the food was ready. Paola helped Ma set the table and bring the food to be served. It was time to call the boys.

Ma yelled out, "¡Panzón! ¡Milito! Cena![1] Dinner time!"

Normally there was no need for a second call for dinner. When dinner was ready, two sets of footsteps would be heard coming down the hallway or rushing through the door from outside. With a whirlwind, the boys would hit their seats at the

---

1   Dinner

table. However, today there was only one boy landing at the dinner table.

After a quick spin coming out of the hallway, Milo rushed in, set his football at his feet and sat down.

"Where's Panzón? Is he OK? Is he sick?" Ma asked, surprised that Epi wasn't the first to arrive at the dinner table.

As he looked through the forks on the table for <u>his</u> fork; everyone had a favorite fork in the family, Milo answered, "No, Ma, he's not sick. He's coming, I think. He's still studying." Seeing Ma's face, he quickly changed the subject, "Where's Pao-Pao?"

Ma scolded him, "Don't call your sister that. You know no le gusta.[2] Paola is getting ready for work at the movie theater. She'll be here to eat then she has to go." Ma turned to Pop. "Ay, Señor,[3] go get him please. La comida[4] is getting cold."

Pop, smiled, and said, "OK Hon."

Pop shouted out to Epi, as he walked down the hall, "Mijo! It's dinner time. What are you doing?"

He arrived at the boys' room and saw Epi on his bed. Pop asked him "¿No me oistes?"[5]

"Sorry, Pop. I heard you. I am just trying to finish this page."

"What is this?" he asked as he looked at Epi's book. "The dictionary?" Pop scratched his head "Oh, its spelling bee time again, yeah? Milo told me you were studying hard."

---

2   She doesn't like it.
3   Mister, or sir
4   The food
5   You didn't hear me?

"Yeah Pop. For the last two years, I've gotten to the final round, and I miss one word and William doesn't—He wins, I lose." Epi hung his head, as if already defeated.

Pop sensed his son's frustration. He knew Epi needed some encouragement. "Mijo, you win your weekly quizzes by getting A's. You win your class competition, and you win the first rounds in the spelling bee. We are always very proud of you."

"I know, Pop. I just want to show everyone I can finish the whole thing." Epi dropped his chin into his hands.

"OK mijo," acknowledged Pop, who thought for a moment. He began again, "Do you remember the book you were telling me about the other day? The one about the boy, named Johnny[6] who hurt himself working on a silver plate or something like that?"

Epi looked up from his dictionary and corrected his Pop, "It was a silver sugar basin."

"Por su puesto.[7] Anyway, didn't you tell me he spent too much time trying to be better than everyone else? And you said he got hurt trying to finish that basin when he wasn't supposed to?"

Epi nodded.

Pop continued, "There's nothing wrong with working hard to be good at what you do, but not when you can hurt yourself doing it. I know it's important to you. But you're not playing with your friends. You're not riding your bike. You're not yourself. Think about that, ok?"

---

6   Forbes, Esther. *Johnny Tremain*. Houghton Mifflin, 1943.
7   Of course

Epi listened to his words. He thought for a minute then closed his book. He lifted his head and smiled. He set it aside and jumped down from his upper bunk bed.

His Pop put his arm around him and said, "Come and eat. Ma, Paola, and Milo are waiting."

A few days later after school, Boni and the boys gathered at the tables in front of Paco's Tacos. Everyone couldn't contain their excitement. Even Cuatro wearing the taco suit had forgotten his job advertising for his dad's truck. They all surrounded Epi.

"Let me see it Epi," said Travi, jumping up and down.

Trying to contain Travi, Cinco said, "Wait, Travi. He will show you...AFTER he shows ME!" He pushed closer to Epi.

Travi kept edging himself in. Cuatro and Boni were trying to look over Epi's shoulder.

Milo finally came to his brother's rescue, "YA!" with his arms outstretched, "He will show everyone right now. One at a time and, maybe… you can hold it, too."

Milo, like Chief of Security, took the medal from his brother and passed it gently to each friend.

Epi was beaming as his Spelling Bee Champion medal was shown to all his friends. A collection of "Oooos" and "Awwws" came from the gang.

At the head of the line, Cuatro exclaimed, "Wow Epi! That is the bestest medal ever!" He passed the award on to his brother.

Cinco added, "I heard you and William went into the Extra Words round." He gave the medal back to Milo.

"True dat!" exclaimed Milo, "I saw the judges have to go to their folders for the next list...TWICE!" He passed the medal over to Boni.

"Wow, that's impressive, Epi. What word knocked William out?"

Epi and Milo, laughing together, answered in chorus, "E-N-E-R-V-A-T-E-D."

Everyone thought for a minute. Cuatro wondered aloud, "'Enervated? What does that mean?!"

Boni interjected, "It means: 'drained of emotional and intellectual vitality'."

The boys looked at her in shock.

"What? I remembered it from our vocab list," she explained.

Epi told the story:

> *At the end of the regular rounds, William and I were going head-to-head in the Extra Words rounds. After two of those, we had to go to the Championship Lists, you know, the special bonus rounds. We went so far that we got to the 3rd extra list. It was my turn and I spelled 'totalitarianism' correctly. I sat down and heard the judges ask William to step to the mic. I saw him take a deep breath and get up from his chair. He stepped to the front of the stage. The judges told him his word. William asked for the definition. They shared it. He took another deep breath then another. He asked them to use it in a sentence. The second judge said, "After Joseph completed his final exam, he felt very enervated." William nodded. His face got a little red and before the judges could*

ask him to begin... HE FAINTED. He dropped right into the arms of Mr. Clayton sitting near him!

Everyone gasped.

Boni clasped her hand over her mouth, "Was he ok?"

"Whoa!" said Cinco.

Cuatro followed with, "Poor guy. That must've been tough on him."

Travi's reaction was a little different, "Dang!" with a smirk, "I wish I was there to see it!"

Boni hit him on the shoulder. "Ow! I mean, poor William." Travi looked up at Boni and she frowned.

"Yeah, he's fine," continued Epi. "After it was over, I went over to check on him. He was sitting in the audience chairs with his parents. I asked him if he was ok, and he smiled and said yes. His mom said it was because he had been staying up late every night studying. She had been telling him to get rest, but he must have been determined to continue working on his lists."

Boni asked, "Really? Why so much? He always made it seem so easy."

"I know. I thought so, too. His mom told me William saw me in the library that day. He thought since I was studying super hard this year, he felt he needed to, as well." Epi smiled at what she told him next, "His mom said I was the only one William knew could beat him. She said he really liked that about me."

The gang exchanged smiles of pride for Epi and respect for William.

Epi continued, "I told her 'Thank you' and asked if he would be OK? She said he just needs rest. Before he left with his mom and dad, he shook my hand and congratulated me."

Epi smiled big - bigger than he ever had before.

"I always thought William was a cool guy," commented Cuatro.

Jumping up and down again, Travi shouted, "Yeah but Epi's the champion this year!" He high-fived Milo.

"Got that right," as Milo high-fived Travi again. Everyone cheered!

"Thanks, everyone." Epi told the gang. "Come on. Let's go to Big Pa's Corner Store. He said he'd give us all GIANT popsicles to celebrate."

Everyone cheered again and gathered their bikes to go. They all waved their goodbyes to Paco, still working in the taco truck.

Cuatro shouted out to his dad, "Bye, Papi. Me and Cinco are going with Epi. We'll be back later."

"Later mijos."

"Bye, Papi," shouted Cinco then turned to his brother. He yelled at him, "Cuatro! Take off that taco suit!"

As he rode behind Cinco, Cuatro asked, "Why?"

THE END

EPI-logue

This work has been a long, labor of love. These stories represent my childhood—growing up with great friends, my family—the center of my world, my neighborhood—where I experienced life and learned so much, and my culture—the essence of who I am and who I grew up to be.

The beauty of this book rests on the broad shoulders of Epifanio, *El Panzón*. He represents all well-fed kids out there having fun and making friends. His eclectic gang of friends mirror my own growing up. They taught me so much and I cherish each adventure.

Thank you for reading and riding your bike along with Epi and his friends.

¡Hasta Luego y Orale!

MARCIANO FLORES
The original Panzón!

Appendix

Epi's Reading List #1

- <u>D'Aulaires' Book of Greek Myths</u> by Ingri and Edgar D'Aulaire
- <u>The Adventures of Sherlock Holmes</u> by Sir Arthur Conan Doyle
- <u>Romeo & Juliet</u> by William Shakespeare
- <u>The House on Mango Street</u> by Sandra Cisneros
- <u>G'Morning/ G'Night</u> by Lin-Manuel Miranda
- <u>The Hobbit</u> by J. R. R. Tolkien
- <u>The Circuit</u> by Francisco Jimenez
- <u>Johnny Tremain</u> by Esther Forbes

MA'S ENCHILADA RECIPE
(with Epi & Milo's Pie version)

Ingredients
- ✓ 1 can enchilada sauce- 28oz (mild, medium, or hot; to taste)
- ✓ 1 lb. of shredded cheddar cheese
- ✓ 8 corn tortillas (serves 4) ; 16 if you are making Enchilada Pie (serves 5-6)
- ✓ 1 lb. of cooked ground beef (or other desired meat)
- ✓ Vegetable or canola oil for frying tortillas

Instructions
- Heat oil for frying in small frying pan
- Heat enchilada sauce in small soup pot
- Using tongs, soft fry each corn tortilla; not crispy like a taco, not soft like a "street taco"
- Rolled:
  - Pre-heat oven to 350 degrees
  - Dip each tortilla in warm enchilada sauce, using tongs
  - Place in medium-size baking pan (usually a 13"x9" pan)
  - Add shredded cheese (and cooked meat)

- Bring full tortilla into rolls, place in pan next to each other
- Once all 8 enchiladas are done, add more cheese on top of all, and pour extra sauce over.
- Bake for 20 minutes or until all are warm and cheese is melted.
- SERVE AND ENJOY with arroz (Mexican rice)!

- Epi's & Milo's Enchilada Pie
  - Pre-heat oven to 350 degrees
  - Dip each tortilla in warm enchilada sauce, using tongs
  - Place in medium-size baking pan across the bottom (usually a 13"x9" pan)
  - Add shredded cheese (and cooked meat) across this first layer
  - Continue this process to make 3-4 more layers
  - Once all layers are done, add more cheese on top, and pour extra sauce over.
  - Bake for 20 minutes or until warm and cheese is melted.
  - Cut into square portions.
  - SERVE AND ENJOY with arroz (Mexican rice)!

About the Author

MARCIANO FLORES grew up a Panzoncito (a little chubby kid). These stories are connected to the fun he had as a child with friends and family, throughout his culture and neighborhood. Marciano has been an educator for the past 25 years. In that time, he has told and re-told these stories of his childhood to his students. He has finally written them to share with all of you.

Made in the USA
Las Vegas, NV
13 April 2023